Lunch Break

Short Stories & Poems

The fiction of Quent Cordair
resides at ~

"As It Should Be"

quentcordair.com

Lunch Break

Short Stories & Poems

Quent Cordair

Cordair Inc.
Napa MMXII

"A Prelude to Pleasure"
First published in 1991 by the Atlantean Press.
Kindle e-book published in 2011 by Cordair Inc.

"April's Justice"
First published in 1994 by the Atlantean Press,
The Atlantean Press Review

"The Whistler"
First published in 1994 by the Atlantean Press,
The Atlantean Press Review

"The Seduction of Santi Banesh"
First published in 1994 by the Atlantean Press,
The Atlantean Press Review
Kindle e-book published in 2011 by Cordair Inc.

"For the Woman Who Has Everything"
First published in 1996 in ART Ideas.

"The Sculpture That Won the War"
First published in 2001 by Quent Cordair Fine Art.

"The Hunter"
First published in 1992 by the Atlantean Press,
The Atlantean Press Review

"Sheltered"
Kindle e-book published in 2011 by Cordair Inc.
Paperback published in 2012 by CreateSpace.

Previously published stories have been lightly revised
and edited for this edition.

ISBN-13: 978-1477683521
ISBN-10: 1477683526

Cordair Inc.
1301 First St., Napa, CA 94559
(707) 255-2242   www.cordair.com

To my wife and best friend,
Linda,
who makes it possible.

Contents

Preface ix

Stories
Poems

My Pledge 2

A Prelude to Pleasure 3

Holding Your Hand 29

April's Justice 30

The Line 44

The Whistler 45

Your Hands 49

The Seduction of Santi Banesh 50

Priceless 67

In My World 68

For the Woman Who Has Everything 69

The Sculpture That Won the War 74

For My Softest One 80

Suite Boxes 82

The Hunter 83

Clever Girl 102

Sheltered 103

About the Author 132

Preface

The *Lunch Break* collection includes work dating back to my very first story, crafted while waiting tables by day and working the graveyard shift in the mail room of a record company. At the time, I was living in the basement of my aunt and uncle's home in Indianapolis, with my aunt's daycare operating directly overhead. The dust from the children's stomping and running filtered down through the glow from my word-processor as I wrote "A Prelude to Pleasure." The story was published by the Atlantean Press in 1991. "April's Justice," "The Hunter," "The Seduction of Santi Banesh" and "The Whistler" were subsequently published in the *Atlantean Press Review,* bolstering my confidence and resolve to persevere. My sincerest thanks to Patricia LeChevalier, publisher of Atlantean Press, wherever she now may be.

After moving to California, I took up painting to support the writing. "For the Woman Who Has Everything" was first published by Alexandra York in *ART Ideas* in 1996, the year in which I opened an art gallery, Quent Cordair Fine Art, to support the painting, to support the writing. With my wife now managing the gallery, my focus is turned, finally and fully, to creating fiction.

The poems, offered as interludes between the stories, were not originally intended for publication, but these diary entries and odes to romantic interests have been as much a part of my creative output as have been my stories and paintings, and I hope that the reader will enjoy them as much as I've enjoyed digging them out of the musty notebooks and exposing them anew to the light of day.

The opening poem, "My Pledge," was composed as I stood at the dawn of my artistic career, determined and with a singular end in mind. Over the years, in my writing, my painting, and in representing the work of our fine painters and sculptors in the gallery, I have held to the purpose as declared in the poem. I'm pleased with the results to date.

Most of the stories and poems have been at least lightly edited from their original form—polished and buffed for the occasion—but all retain their original character and structure, with touch-ups being mostly cosmetic.

The cover art for this edition, my painting *Lunch Break*, was chosen because its theme complements the idea for the collection: each of the stories may be fully enjoyed within the span of a lunch hour, as a brief and uplifting respite from one's daily efforts. Further, the painting's theme complements the metaphysical orientation of the stories—the conviction and reaffirmation that this earth is a place where we belong, that ours is a benevolent, rewarding universe for anyone who chooses to pursue happiness with integrity, passion and perseverance.

I will be forever grateful for the generous hospitality extended by my Uncle Ted and Aunt Doreen during a time in my life in which I was, from one perspective, at a low point, both literally and figuratively, but from another, in a position that proved to be an invaluable opportunity to find my grounding and to start anew.

Thanks to Allegra Durante and Dianne Durante, my copy editors nonpareil. Many improvements and corrections in this volume are to their credit. Any residual flaws are my own.

Thanks to my wife, Linda, for her steadfast love, indefatigable support, and helpful suggestions along the way. Without her, this publication would not be in your hands.

Thanks to my fans, who have been so wonderfully generous and encouraging with their reviews and their expressed longings for more to read—they continue to keep me refueled and optimistic.

Finally, that this edition is not dedicated to Ayn Rand is only due to my desire to reserve that recognition for a future work. I should say here, however, that nothing has inspired my work more than Ms. Rand's fiction and non-fiction, particularly *A Romantic Manifesto*, a work which I would encourage all aspiring writers and artists to explore and study for its approach to creating and analyzing stylized, meaningful art. The reader familiar with Ms. Rand and her philosophy, Objectivism, might note a tip of the cap or two in this collection. I owe her much credit for any strengths in my writing and vision and no blame for any weaknesses. To this day, I regret never having met the remarkable woman—she passed away in March of 1982, only months before I discovered her work.

Quent Cordair
June 11, 2012

Lunch Break

My Pledge

From the gray I will forge
The black and the white,
From pale hue, a brilliant spectrum,
A line without bend,
A view to the end
Of our glory and ecstasy,
Of the world
As it could and should be.

A Prelude to Pleasure

GARRETT BRACE WAS SOARING seven miles above the earth, flying faster than sound. When the snowcapped Rockies came sharply into focus, he pulled the wheel back with one finger, pushed the throttle in with another and sent his plane climbing toward a wall of dark thunderclouds. The white machine sliced neatly through them and shot out into an empty blue sky, where below, there was only a carpet of cottony cumulus stretching away to the distant horizon.

"Okay, Pete, she's yours," he said, to the pilot beside him. "According to the weather reports, it should be smooth sailing from here to New York." But he sat for a moment longer, letting his hands rest on the controls until he felt the cool metal warming to the heat of his touch. He smiled: it was a fine plane, the best that money could buy.

Pete had been watching him. "Garrett, you should have been a pilot yourself—but back during World War I. I keep seeing you in goggles, scarf and a leather jacket."

Garrett chuckled softly. He was a quiet man with dark, wavy hair; his eyes were always thinking, often laughing.

"Okay, Pete, she's yours."

He relinquished the controls and was stepping through the door to the cabin when he hesitated, trying to place the woman who sat by the window reading a magazine. The cushions seemed made to fit the body beneath her loose-fitting clothes; her smooth, exquisite face was remarkably void of a distinguishing characteristic.

"Oh . . . hello, Celeste," he said after a moment. "You look comfortable."

"I am, darling, thank you. Can I get you a drink? . . . Or is there anything else I can do for you?"

"No . . . no, I have work to do," he answered, holding the smile.

"Of course, dear. I'll be right here."

He walked past her and sat down at his desk, where he remained motionless, trying not to think. There was a faint brown ring on the otherwise spotless surface. As he traced it with his finger, his smile faded. The stain was from his last cup of coffee, and he rubbed it without effect. The ring itself was too minor a detail to bother him, but the only thing he could associate it with was the ring in his pocket; he could feel the sharp edge of its stone pressing into his leg. There was nothing about *that* ring that could possibly cause concern: he had spent five years making sure of it.

He sighed and pressed a switch on the desk. His shoulders relaxed as the soft hum of the computer joined the quiet whine of the jet engines. After adjusting the monitors in front of him, his fingers found the keyboard and began tapping out an intricate rhythm. Screens of graphs, charts, and columns of figures appeared, merged, changed and disappeared on command. Every detail was a vital statistic of a business concern somewhere on the earth below. Garrett Brace was in his element. He soon forgot Celeste Warren and the ring.

An hour later he was studying a bill for repairs to drilling equipment on a Texas oil field when he stopped: the price of o-rings had gone up again. He glared at the ring of coffee stain. But maybe it wasn't the ring part that bothered him. . . . Could it be the *coffee*? He couldn't think of any recent economic or political changes in the coffee-exporting countries that might affect one of his shipping lines. There was no crop-threatening hurricane brewing. There had been no significant change in the supply or demand. But if it wasn't the coffee, and it wasn't the ring . . . it was the *stain*!

He struck two keys—the oil company disappeared—and with three keys more he summoned the file of a small New Jersey chemical company. He had reviewed the company only the day before, finding nothing abnormal at the time, but now he quickly narrowed his focus to the minutes of the last board meeting and to the briefing by the head of the research and development department. He found what he was looking for. Without moving his eyes from the screen, he mashed a button on the desk.

"Helen, get Dr. Kilgor on the line!" There was no answer. "Helen . . . ?"

He remembered it was Saturday—his secretary below wasn't working. Throwing open a desk drawer, he scattered its contents, found a dog-eared notebook and leafed furiously through the pages. His finger stopped on a phone number which he punched into the keyboard.

A little girl's voice answered shyly, "Hello?"

"Cindy? May I speak with your father, please?"

"Daddy's not home right now. He's at work making something very special. But Mommy's here. Do you want to—?"

"No thanks, honey." Garrett disconnected, cursing, and found the number for the research laboratory at J & G Chemical. No one answered there. He stayed on the line, waiting, using the time to examine the cold, raw dread that was rising into his chest and sinking into his legs. Its seed had been the slight irritation at the coffee stain. He knew the progression well.

"Hello?" came a voice over the phone.

"Dr. Kilgor?"

"Mr. Brace! A pleasure to hear from you, sir. What can I do for you today?"

You just did it, Garrett thought, breathing a sigh of relief. "Tell me about the wood-stain formula you're working on."

"How did you know . . . ? Oh yes, well, I suppose you would. Anyway, as I mentioned in my report, I think we can cut the cost of producing the stain nearly in half by—"

"I read all of that. Give me the formulas."

The scientist did and concluded: "I'll have it ready for testing in about an hour, Mr. Brace. Do you want me to call you back with the result?"

"That wouldn't be necessary, Dr. Kilgor. I could probably hear it from here."

"What?"

"Eighteen years ago your predecessor was brewing the same

concoction, and fortunately, he stepped out of the lab for a cup of coffee. Take a look at the west wall. See the difference from the others? . . . Of course, rebuilding the wall was the least of the expense—I shudder at the thought of having to replace all the new equipment we installed for you last year—and besides, it might take me more than a day or two to replace *you*, Steve."

"Christ! I was about to . . . if you hadn't . . ." The scientist's voice dropped away and there was a moment of silence. "Thanks, Garrett."

"You can thank me by having the details of the new plastic worked out by the end of the month. I have a research firm in Concord working on a biotech application for it, and I'm upgrading the systems at three manufacturing plants to accommodate production as soon as it's ready, so do me a favor—stay in one piece long enough to finish it, okay? . . . By the way, how's the baby?"

"Growing so fast I can't keep clothes on him." There was a smile in his voice. "I'm going to have to invent a material that will grow with him . . . but later—I've got work to do."

"Good to hear it, Dr. Kilgor. Have a good weekend."

"You too, Mr. Brace."

Garrett spent another hour studying companies and subsidiaries. He had owned several of them for nearly twenty years, two had been acquired only four days ago, but all were given the same attention and care; each had to be maintained, nurtured, cultivated and made to grow. When he touched the keyboard, his nerve endings leapt out to the corners of his empire sensing every nut and bolt of every beam and pipe of every factory, warehouse, office and store. As the plane shifted course, a band of warm sunlight fell across its owner's chest.

Turning to the financial and political news, he found nothing that required action. There was a heightened sensation at the back of his neck and the lines of his body pulled taut as he leaned forward in his chair: it was time for his favorite work.

Five localities had been carefully selected for the day's hunt. He began the search in a small city in Kentucky, methodically scanning the headlines and articles of the local news services. A store opening, a corporate merger, a hole in a market, a new product—anything might trigger that little—he hadn't found a name for it, but the sensation was the opposite and complement of the one he had felt at the coffee stain—it was a nudge, a whispered hint of possibility, a tiny prelude to pleasure. Usually, as he would follow a lead, the trail would disappear as additional data eliminated the prospect from further consideration. But sometimes . . . every once in a while . . .

He searched on, moving on to the second city, then to the third. The daily hunts had been unsuccessful for three weeks now, and once again there was much worth noting, but nothing of immediate value, nothing that he could act on or that might—

There . . .

Tucked away in the "Life & Style" section of the Phoenix Sun Times was a three-paragraph article which tangentially mentioned a regional toy retailer that was launching a small fleet of converted school busses. The mobile playroom-stores would make regularly scheduled visits to the surrounding neighborhoods and could be booked for parties and events. When available, they would travel to any home immediately upon a parent's or grandparent's request. Garrett smiled.

He jumped to his reference resources and found the current financial report on Dream Toys of Phoenix. Their bottom line was low, but their fundamentals were sturdy. Garrett pulled the sum of his knowledge and perspicacity into a white-hot focus and brought it all to bear upon the available facts, which gradually revealed—potential. Great potential if the concept were to be expanded into additional markets nationwide. A tingling numbness coursed through his wrists and palms. Monday morning, he would find the owner, make him an irresistible offer—and buy another company.

Garrett leaned back in the chair and looked out at the cold blue sky and the endless stretch of clouds. He had made a fortune doing just what he was doing now, what he most loved to do. His eyes fell on the wing's sharp metal edge and followed it in through the window to the clean, efficient lines of the cabin. The joy of another small victory was building within him and begging for the release of a champagne cork and the crowning ecstasy of making love to—he watched Celeste smoothly turn a page of the magazine. He straightened in his chair—and went back to work.

He found who owned Dream Toys of Phoenix: it was the Strive Company. Slamming his fist on the desk made his computer screens blink and flash with unintelligible characters. In the past months he had tried twice to buy Strive subsidiaries, but in reply to his repeated inquiries he had received only a terse, handwritten note on the company's letterhead stating:

"I don't sell unless it is first my idea to do so. What I have is good—and I know it." The words were Garrett's own, quoted from a rare interview. The note was signed only, "The Strive Company."

He had ripped the note to shreds, knowing that it wasn't the message or the writer that infuriated him—he was angry with himself: it should have been *his* signature on that letterhead; *he* should have owned the Strive Company. He could have—but instead . . .

He reached slowly for the keyboard and deliberately typed, "B-L-A-I-N."

Five months before, on an icy January morning, he had been in Manhattan arranging the financing to purchase the Strive Company. As he was walking by the bustling entrance of an office building, a hand shot out of the crowd. It belonged to Phillip Warren, Celeste's brother.

"Garrett! How good to see you! Come on up and have a cup of coffee." Phillip's handsomeness was a serviceable shade of his sister's beauty, his impeccable black attire was offset with a casual air.

Garrett couldn't devise an excuse quickly enough to save himself from being deftly ushered to a top-floor office with a view of the skyline and harbor. After closing the door behind them, Phillip descended into a high-backed leather chair behind a wide mahogany desk which was cleared of everything save a black pen; its embedded diamond twinkled as Phillip positioned the instrument within reach of his right hand. On the wall behind him hung a set of three diplomas from the most prestigious business schools in the country.

"Have a seat, old friend," Phillip said, motioning to the room's only other chair, which faced the desk. The two had met only once before.

"Frankly, I'm glad you stopped by the neighborhood," he continued, a twist playing at the corner of his smile. "It saves me the trouble of tracking you down. I have something I've been wanting to show you." He pulled a manila folder from the desk drawer.

Garrett winced. Phillip Warren was reputed to be one of the better traders in Manhattan. If he could corner Garrett Brace, he was on his way to becoming one of the best.

"Listen, Phillip," Garrett said patiently, "I know where this is going and it's no use: buying and running businesses *is* my business. *I* find what I like, *I* set the terms, and then I buy. No one has ever sold me a business and no one ever will. So let's not waste our time—come on, I'll buy you lunch."

"Give me just five minutes—and I'll buy *you* lunch," Phillip said evenly; his smile was all but gone and he was too confident, as if he knew something Garrett didn't. Reluctantly, Garrett decided to stay, to find out what that something was.

"What I have in this folder"—Phillip placed it on the desk between them—"is a contract for the purchase of three million shares of the Blain Corporation, at an excellent price. You know what the company is and what those shares represent: the Blain Corporation is one of the largest, best organized, most meticulously managed, most carefully diversified companies in the world; the three million shares are valued at roughly a quarter of your net worth. Now, we could sit here all day and argue the pros, cons and details—but I'll save you the trouble . . ." He leaned forward and, with no expression on his face, looked Garrett in the eye; his voice dropped to just above a whisper.

"I'm a salesman, Garrett. My job is reading men. I've been watching you for a long time, and lately, something's been bothering me. . . .

"I happen to know that you spent a lot of time and money searching for the *perfect* woman to be your bride—and you found my sister, Celeste, right? . . . That's okay, you don't have to answer. You wouldn't spend your love on anything less than the best, would you? Well, that's just good business—and you're a damned good businessman. Which brings me to the point: I've finally figured out what's been bothering me, Garrett: it's the inconsistency, the inconsistency in an otherwise exceptionally consistent man. I'm sure it's simply an oversight on your part, and I'm pleased to be in a position to help."

Garrett wanted to spring from the chair and fly from the room, through the window if necessary—but he couldn't move.

". . . And now that I'm offering you the opportunity, my friend, I'm confident that you will put aside any irrelevant emotional whims—and invest your *wealth* as wisely, and as carefully, as you've invested your *heart*."

Phillip opened the folder and slid it gently to the front of the desk, placing the pen on the paper. There was an "X" beside the signature line. Then he sat back in the chair, his expression still blank, and he watched Garrett, whose eyes had dropped to the contract.

Neither of the men moved or spoke.

Five minutes later, as though someone had restarted a film that had been paused mid-scene, Garrett leaned forward, picked up the pen and signed his name.

"Contact my bank the day after tomorrow," he said flatly. "The funds will be transferred to your firm's account. Good day, Mr. Warren." He stood abruptly, turned, and walked to the door.

Phillip called after him, "Hey, Garrett—we're still going out to lunch, aren't we? It's on me. . . ."

But Garrett was already gone.

"Are you finished working, darling?" Celeste asked, laying the magazine aside.

"I hope not."

From Phillip's office Garrett had driven directly to the airport and had left, alone, for a two-week vacation in the Caribbean. While he was away, someone else purchased the Strive Company. He hadn't heard from Phillip again, but he knew that he would, and he knew that he still had nothing with which to fight Phillip's logic. The figures on the Blain Corporation sat ponderously on the screen before him. Garrett hadn't gotten involved in its management or board—there was no need.

He turned off the computer and went to lie down on the cushions beside Celeste, his forehead dropping onto the back of his hands. As she bent over him and massaged his shoulders, he surrendered to the weariness that had come over him, the weariness he had felt with increasing frequency since the vacation. He was only forty-five years old.

Her hands moved to his back, where they gently and firmly kneaded his tight muscles.

Five years ago, Garrett had hired two psychologists, three demographers and a firm of private investigators. He had given the team a detailed list of character traits, attributes, mannerisms and physical qualities, with which they had methodically and scientifically scoured the country and the world. Three years later, they had handed him a list of the fifty women who best fit the specifications. The skills of a polished, irresistibly handsome actor had then uncovered the more subtle details, cutting the number to six. Garrett had personally courted each of the finalists, and a year ago to the day, he had narrowed his attention to one.

Celeste Warren was intelligent, refined, witty and honest, with a statuesque body to match her flawless face. Her family had enough money that she wasn't enamored of his, and she was devoted to him from the day they first met. She was like a kitten around him—warm and affectionate, but happy to amuse herself for as long as he was otherwise occupied. One evening over candlelight, she had confessed being in love with him—so Garrett secretly offered three notoriously successful playboys a staggering reward for the first who could induce any infidelity in her. She hadn't wavered.

"What are you wearing to the wedding, darling?" she asked softly. Her hands had moved down to his legs.

"What?"

"I'm sorry, dear, had you fallen asleep?"

"Wedding? Who said anything about a wedding?"

"Phil's wedding," she reproached lightly. "Remember, we're flying to my brother's wedding?"

"Yes . . . yes, of course. . . . Well, what am I supposed to wear?"

"Blue. The family is wearing blue."

"Blue it is then."

Garrett shut his eyes—she was patiently awaiting his proposal, knowing it would come, as surely as he knew what her answer would be. The engagement ring, now wedged between his leg and the cushion, was set with a Blain diamond—out of no loyalty to the company—Blain simply had the best diamonds.

The steady massaging was putting him to sleep. Celeste leaned over and kissed him lightly on the back of the neck. Rising, she took his hand and led him to the bedroom in the rear of the plane where he lay down again, a pillow propped behind his head. She closed the door silently, and holding his eyes with her own, she undressed slowly, as casually as she would have alone, and stood silently before him, naked. The sunlight pouring in from the windows left no shadow on her flawless ivory body.

When her body moved again, she was coming to sit beside him. Her fingers slipped beneath his shirt to brush across his skin, and he allowed her to undress him, skillfully caressing him all the while, sensing his body the way she sensed his mind, reacting with what he wanted, in the degree that he wanted it. Lying down beside him, she guided him to her.

It had been twenty years since he had made love to a woman.

Before the five-year search there had been fifteen long years of watching and waiting to fall passionately in love the way he always believed he would, the way he once thought he had. But on his fortieth birthday, he stood alone on a rock above a restless ocean and cried. There was no one with whom to share his world, and there seemed to be nothing he could do about it. In business he could do anything, achieve anything, he refused to accept failure—but he couldn't create a woman, and he couldn't fall in love with one who simply wasn't there. Lifting his head, he had angrily wiped away the tears: he had been more than patient with the world, and the world hadn't delivered on its promise. And if he couldn't have what he wanted—he swore he would get the best that could be had. Five years later, he was in bed with Celeste Warren, and he couldn't make love to her.

"I'm sorry," he said.

"Don't worry about it, darling," she answered soothingly, resuming the massage. "You've had a long day, and you're tense from your work—just relax."

"Excuse me." He got up and went into the bathroom, closing the door behind him. His hands were shaking; he gripped the sides of the sink. Then he turned on the water because he didn't want Celeste, the best that could be had, to hear that he was sick..

In the heart of an exclusive suburb on the north side of the city, the Warren residence had been built with a careful eye to a balance between luxury and restraint. From the many fine cars in the drive, it appeared that a party had gathered there after the wedding-rehearsal dinner. Garrett and Celeste were met at the door by Mrs. Candice Warren.

"Darling!" She exchanged a brushing kiss with her daughter. The two were often mistaken for sisters.

"Good evening, Mother. You remember my friend, Mr. Garrett Brace."

"Why, I couldn't possibly forget such a handsome gentleman. And what a splendid couple you make."

"Thank you, Mrs. Warren," Garrett answered. "And you are as lovely as always."

"You are too gracious—it fades with time. But come, I shouldn't be selfish with you. Celeste, your brother won't feel the evening is complete without your best wishes." She led them into the high-ceilinged parlor. "This was so unexpected, you know—Phillip getting married, and on such short notice. It's not like him at all. Of course I'm completely happy for him—he needs a woman in his life. But first, your father. I'm sure he is eager to see you, dear."

They made their way through the well-arranged groupings of people and furnishings to a somber, quiet corner of the room where a heavy chair sat in a cone of lamplight. The edge of the light cut down and across Harold Warren's robe-encased body; his head was in shadow.

"My God, Celeste," the voice from the chair called out, "you are a vision. If your mother were not the saint that she is, I would swear that your father was Apollo himself. Let me look at you." As he spoke, only his eyes and lips moved.

"You remember Mr. Garrett Brace, father."

"I've heard of a Brace who's some sort of hotheaded, pretentious billionaire"—he squinted, examining Garrett with suspicion—"are you any relation to him?"

"Father, Mr. Brace was here at last year's Christmas party."

"Oh? . . . Oh, yes . . . you *are* that billionaire, aren't you? I used to be rich too, you know. I was . . . one of the best . . ."

"But you still are, love," his wife said gently. "You're worth three times what you were when you worked so hard at it."

"That's why I need you to help me out of bed in the morning and why our son controls our finances, isn't it?—because I'm worth three times what I used to be?" His eyes turned again on Garrett.

"So what do you want, young man? It's not Christmas again yet, is it? If you're wanting me to buy into some visionary venture of yours, go and talk to my son." He looked down at the hands lying in his lap. "I don't bother with it anymore."

"Harold, love," his wife said, "Celeste and I will be in the kitchen. We have some catching up to do." She glanced at her daughter knowingly. "Garrett, please make yourself at home, and after the two of you are reacquainted, I'll have Phillip introduce you around."

"I'm not senile yet, woman," Harold snapped. "I remember him perfectly well now."

"Of course, darling. I'll be back with your medication in twenty minutes." She bent over and kissed him on his pale, balding head. "I love you," she said.

As mother and daughter glided away across the polished floor, Harold Warren's chin dropped to his chest. Garrett stood alone before him.

"She's told me that a million times," the old man muttered, "and I still have to believe her. She's the same woman she was the day I met her, the same woman I married, the same woman to whom I've been married for thirty-five years."

"She is extraordinary, sir, and I compliment you both for having raised your daughter to be just like her."

"Those two are . . . exquisite, aren't they." He raised his eyes, following the line of Garrett's body.

"You, young man, are one of a hundred who have wanted to marry Celeste—please, it's obvious enough—and you're probably the most qualified of the lot. But I don't interfere with her life. Her mother has trained her well—she can take care of herself. You'll get no resistance from me."

"Thank you, Mr. Warren."

"Don't thank me, Mr. Brace. I'm letting you make the worst mistake of your life. You're not in love with her and you know it. You couldn't be—you're too much like me . . . like I was. Look at me, Mr. Garrett Brace, Mr. Ruler of the World, look at me. I once ruled it myself. On my wedding day I took a sedative so I could stand through the ceremony, and I've been taking them ever since. I'm getting numb. The feeling now ends at my knees, and look—" he held out his arms where atrophied hands dangled from his wrists—"nothing. They feel nothing. Look at me, how old do you think I am? I know how old you are: you're forty-five. You'll be forty-six on the ninth of August. Well, I'm only ten years older than you, and I may have to live another ten before I die."

With all his strength he leaned over the side of the chair and flailed at the lamp. On the third effort he knocked it to the floor where it shattered, leaving him completely in shadow.

"Go ahead . . . marry her," he rasped as he struggled to breathe. "She's . . . the best . . . you'll find. . . ."

Garrett's eyes riveted on the gold-embroidered "H.W." that rose and fell on the dying man's chest.

At the commotion, Phillip had come walking too steadily from the bar. He picked up the bigger pieces of the lamp.

"Don't mind him—he's always been this way. He was throwing things at me before I was big enough to dodge them. You'll get used to him though. He's harmless."

Harold Warren stared at the floor in silence.

"Come on, Garrett, you look like you could use a drink." Phillip took his arm and led him to the bar. He ordered for them both and laid his hand heavily on Garrett's shoulder.

"So, how's business, old friend? That Blain stock isn't so bad now, is it? It's high quality stuff—like this liquor. Your system just has to adjust to it, that's all. No other company grows more dependably. The Blain Corporation is without question one of the highest quality, best organized, most . . . Do you know I'm getting married tomorrow? Can hardly believe it myself. . . . And when the honeymoon stuff is over and I'm back in town, I want you to come up to my office because I've got another little secret I want to share with you before anyone else. . . ."

Garrett was already on his second drink, his mind twenty years away.

He had fallen in love with the actress the first time he saw her on the movie screen. They were married two weeks after he had invested heavily in the production company she was filming for, and for the next two months he was in a heaven of cool white sheets and drenching, draining worship. While he was in heaven, she was surreptitiously liquidating most of his assets and using the rest for collateral. It was a sizeable fortune—she was a good actress. Then she disappeared, leaving him with the three hundred dollars in his wallet. Three years later she was found lying next to the body of a Central American dictator who had been killed in a bloody coup. She was dead, the money was gone. There was nothing for Garrett to do but to rebuild his fortune—and wait again for the response he had felt and for the love that he thought he had found.

He was on his fourth drink, staring into a puddle of yellow liquid that Phillip had spilled on the bar. The lines in the puddle's reflection swirled and changed and formed a shimmering "H.W." Pushing the drink away, he shook his head to clear the image. When he looked again, the letters had changed to "G.B."

He was halfway across the room before his teetering chair hit the floor. There was a musty, rotting smell of old clothes in the place, and he desperately wanted to find fresh air. The closest exit was into a darkened hallway. The doors along each side were closed, but there was a turn at the end. When he reached the corner, he stopped and looked back at the pale rectangle of light that was the parlor—then he turned and made his way into the darkness.

His vision adjusted enough to make out, at the passage's end, a pair of heavy double doors with a line of blue light emanating from their bottom edge. Coming faintly from within was what sounded like—a symphony. He tried the handles and pulled one of the doors open slowly. Music and light spilled out around him. Scrolling on a large screen on the opposite wall were the opening credits of an old black-and-white film. The room was a small theatre. Garrett smiled: the movie had been one of his favorites when he was growing up. He hadn't seen it since.

At first it appeared he was alone in the room, but squinting his eyes, he made out the top of a ruffled head of hair in the middle of the rows of seats. Closing the door quietly behind him, he made his way down the aisle to discover that the head belonged to a boy not more than eleven or twelve years old. He was sitting cross-legged with a bowl of popcorn in his lap. When Garrett sat down beside him, the boy, without taking his eyes from the screen, passed the bowl.

"Thanks."

"Shhh."

The movie was about a woman whose mission it was to find a cunning enemy agent, to seduce him and to kill him. There was little known about the man, not even his name. Armed only with a blurred photograph, a small handgun and her determination, she tracked and pursued him all over the world, always coming within just a few moments or a few steps of seeing him. As she learned his every habit and motivation, she became increasingly captivated, and driven as much by a need to see his face as by the necessity of completing her task. Finally, she followed him into a remote desert, certain that he wouldn't be able to elude her there—but she became hopelessly lost. Overcome by exhaustion and the burning heat, she fell to the sand.

Lifting her eyes, she saw him on the crest of the dune above her, traced against the white desert sky. Pulling herself to her knees, she drew the gun and aimed . . . but her hands began to shake. She wiped a tear away with her sleeve.

"I'm sorry," she said, "but you see—I've fallen in love with you. . . ." She steadied the gun, closed her eyes, and fired.

When she looked again, he was still standing there. Dropping the gun, she struggled to her feet and stumbled up the dune toward the shimmering figure—but the mirage disappeared. She fell again. Taking the picture from her pocket, she kissed it and whispered, "Maybe you were only a dream—but I loved you." Her hand, still holding the picture, fell, and the blowing sand began to cover her body.

Suddenly, she was being lifted, and she opened her eyes to see that she was being carried up the dune in his arms.

The lines of the closing scene were burned into Garrett's memory. He knew every word by heart.

"It's a good thing you fired your gun—" the man's voice was deep velvet with an Italian accent—"I never would have known you were here. But, tell me, what is such an extraordinary and beautiful woman doing alone in the desert?"

"I'm afraid I was trying to kill you."

"Oh, now that is a very serious crime." His laughing eyes betrayed the stern expression on his face. "You should be severely punished. What should I do to you?"

"You should torture me, or kill me, or abandon me here to die . . . but whatever you do, please don't kiss me."

He stopped walking, looked long into her eyes, and with the sand swirling at his feet, he kissed her.

That was the way the movie ended.

The boy stood, applauding vigorously. "Great movie, isn't it? This is the eighth time I've seen it. Want to watch it again? Or do you want to see a different one? I have—" Garrett smiled as the boy offered a list of movies all older than Garrett himself, each complementing the joy and innocence of the young face.

"No, I really wish I could," Garrett said, "but I have to go. There is . . . something I have to do. Who are you anyway?"

"Michael. Michael Warren. And whom do I have the honor of addressing? Hast thou escaped from the dark side to become a Knight of the Holy Treasure Quest, forever bound to fight the evil forces of Gray Boredom to the end of your days? Or art thou a traitor and a spy who hast simply lost his way to the bathroom? We get those here occasionally, you know."

Garrett liked him. "Sir Michael Warren, I'll have you know that you are addressing a life member of the Holy Treasure Quest, a member of many years—three, nay, four times as many years as you are old."

"But art thou a member in good standing?" the boy asked. "Hast thou been true to the cause? The fact that thou hast just entered from the dark side—probably from my brother's exhilarating party—makes thee highly suspect. What is your name, good sir?"

"Garrett Brace."

"Garrett Brace the billionaire?"

"Yes."

"Hmm—well, by your age you should be. Actually, I'm glad you're here, Mr. Brace. You can answer a question that's been bothering me for some time: I used to think that you were the only businessman out there who really knew what he was doing. I was learning a lot from watching your moves. Then you bought into Blain. Why?"

"Excuse me, but how old are you?"

"Does it matter?"

"No. It's just that you remind me a lot of myself when I was your age. I'll bet you don't get along very well with the rest of this family, do you?"

"Please answer the question, Mr. Brace."

"Well, Michael, the Blain Corporation is one of the largest, best organized, most meticulously managed—"

"Oh, *please!*"

"Michael, it's not like the movies out there in the real world," Garrett said, with an edge of irritation. "It's not a game and it's not always fun. But the desert part is real enough—and if you go wandering into it, chasing after mirages, you'll discover that the heat and the sand and the thirst are real too. You seldom find what you're looking for, and sometimes you're damned lucky if you make it out alive. Wait until you grow up—you'll find out—and I hope you do it a lot faster than I did. You'll learn to settle for what the world gives you and be satisfied with it, like it or not."

"I'd rather die."

"Look, you cocky little—"

"Are you going to marry my sister?"

"What does that have to do with it?"

"Everything."

Garrett didn't answer. He looked over to the blank white screen.

"Traitor." Michael sat down, crossing his arms and facing the front. "My sister and the Blain Corporation—" he said with disgust— "the two most boring things on earth." Pushing a button on the armrest, he dimmed the lights and started another movie.

Garrett marched from the theatre. You don't fall in love with photographs, he fumed, or if you do, the person turns out to be something entirely different from what you fell in love with. You don't hear shots in the desert, and you won't find the woman of your dreams just lying there, waiting for you to rescue her. You won't find her, she's not in the desert, she's not anywhere. She doesn't exist. . . . He had searched for her for twenty years—nearly twice as long as that damned kid had been alive. Well, brash little brothers and crazy old men wouldn't stop him from doing what he had determined to do.

He thrust his hand into his pocket and balled the ring into his fist. By the time he reached the parlor, he was composed, determined, and a little weary. The effects of the alcohol had worn off. The guests were gone, but Celeste was waiting for him. There were two crystal champagne flutes on the coffee table and a bottle on ice, flanked by two lit candles. Looking at his watch, he saw that he had been away for over two hours.

"There you are, darling," she said lightly. "Have you been enjoying yourself?"

"Doing what?"

"Whatever it was you were doing, dear. I've set out some champagne for us. The rest of the family has retired, so we won't be disturbed."

"No . . . I don't suppose we will be. . . ."

They sat on the sofa and Celeste filled the glasses.

"To us—" She raised a toast.

He touched his glass to hers and they drank.

"It's so wonderful that Phillip is finally getting married," she said. "It will settle him. Mother tells me his fiancée comes from a fine family and should fit right in. Phil is going to build a new home for them on a lovely estate in Massachusetts. . . ." Her finger traced the rim of the glass. "Massachusetts is nice, but I prefer your property upstate—you know, near the quaint little town with the white clapboard church and the darling general store. What's the name of the town again?"

It was his cue to start leisurely down the path to proposal. She was making it easy for him.

"Celeste?"

"Yes, Garrett?" She was as confident as her brother had been that day in his office.

"Celeste, will you—" his eyes stopped on the coffee table where her glass had left a wet ring—"will you . . . be offended if I walked back to the hotel rather than take the car? I really could use the fresh air."

"Why, of course not, darling. Do you want me to go with you?" There was no disappointment in her voice.

"No . . . no, that's all right."

She walked him to the door. "Be careful, dear," she said. "Even in this neighborhood, it can be dangerous at night."

Especially in this neighborhood, Garrett thought. There wasn't a breath of wind to move the shadows on the lawn.

"Three o'clock tomorrow?" she asked.

"I'm sorry?"

"Three o'clock. The wedding is at three o'clock."

"Oh, yes, the wedding."

He walked down and out from the shadows and into the well-lighted street, where the only shadow was his own and the only sound was that of his own footsteps echoing from the stone walls that protected the silent houses.

* * *

When he looked up again, the walls and the streetlights were gone. The earth was lit only by silver clouds and a full white moon. He was approaching a massive, towering structure which stood alone across the street from a field of tall grass. It was a cathedral. The twin steeples dropped shadows that ended in crosses, one marking the middle of the street, the other falling on the sidewalk ahead of him. He walked through it and into the cathedral's shadow.

Planted at the base of the facade was a stone slab engraved with the cathedral's name. Garrett recognized it as the place where the wedding would be in a few hours time. As he pondered the steps leading up to what seemed a too-small door, it occurred to him that Mrs. Warren would probably choose this very venue for her daughter's wedding when the time came. He climbed the steps and, finding the door unlocked, went inside.

The narrow vestibule led to a vast auditorium. Here, too, was only the moonlight, but filtered into a dark spectrum by the stained glass above. The center aisle of red carpet had been overlaid with a narrow runner of white which led from his feet to the distant shore of the altar. He tested the path with one foot, then stepped onto it with the other. Fixing his eyes on the altar, he walked steadily forward.

The pews extended out to tall, thin windows that reached to the vaulted ceiling in the darkness above. Centered in an enormous arch of stained glass behind the altar was the figure of a dying man stretched between the earth and sky, eyes strained upward in agony. The altar was covered from wall to wall with flowers in readiness for the wedding. When Garrett reached the altar, he bent down and carefully drew a red rose from one of the arrangements. Bringing it to his lips, he breathed in its fragrance.

"Hello, my love. . . . I hope you'll forgive me for what I'm about to do, but there's no other way. I don't know why I've waited as long as I have. I'm not even sure how I came to love you in the first place. I've never met you. I don't know your name or what you look like. But, you see, the movies and the books and the paintings and the music—they all told me that you exist—and I believed them. Why shouldn't I have believed them? I even thought you came once—

but it was only someone pretending to be you. You never came." The moonlight caught a tear that hesitated on his cheek.

"You see, my love, I live in a real world and I need a real person—a face I can see, laughter I can hear, a body I can touch. But you never came. I can't go on like this forever, can I? . . . should I?"

There was nothing to answer him but the sound of his own heartbeat. He tightened his hand into a fist around the stem of the rose and raised it to the crucifix.

"What are *you* so miserable about? You had nothing to live for." The tears streamed down his face. "You should have had a dream, a true love—and then had to kill her. That's real pain, and it hurts like hell."

The stained light on his face shifted from gold to deep blue. He looked to the rose and loosened his hand to hold it more tenderly. A drop of blood rolled across his wrist and fell to the white carpet.

"Maybe you were only a dream—but I loved you." He let the rose fall, then he turned to face the door and walked away.

On the rose's stem, a second drop of blood appeared at the tip of a thorn, and fell.

The dawn brought a cloudless June Sunday, and Garrett woke early as usual. He ordered a hearty breakfast to be brought to his room and had just finished dressing in his blue suit when a waiter wheeled in the table set with gleaming china and silver. As the young man was leaving, he stopped and stared at the picture of Celeste on the nightstand.

"I beg your pardon, sir, but is that your wife?"

"Not yet."

"That is the most beautiful woman I have ever seen!" He turned to Garrett. "You are a very lucky man, sir."

Garrett tipped him double the customary. After eating every bite of the breakfast, he poured himself a fresh cup of coffee and read all of the Sunday paper. The comics were funnier than usual. The stocks section showed the Blain Corporation having ended the week moving just above the index. The wound in his right palm was healing nicely. He reached for the telephone—today would be business as usual.

"Gino? . . . Good morning, my friend. I want you to set my table for two this evening, and bring in that string quintet. . . . I know it's short notice—pay them whatever's necessary. And also, my companion and I will be your only guests this evening. . . . I don't care how many reservations you have. The last time I checked, I owned the place and you worked for me. . . . Yes, thank you, Gino. We'll see you at about seven."

He took the ring from the dresser and peered into the translucent Blain diamond. Tonight, it would be on Celeste Warren's finger.

He turned on the television and watched a documentary on mountain goats, then a show about trout fishing. At the appointed hour, he retraced his steps to the cathedral.

It was a perfectly normal cathedral, not formidable in the least. The grounds were well-manicured. Rows of red and white flowers bordered the walks and the gray stone walls.

The auditorium, already filled with guests, was nearly as bright as the day without. The flower-bedecked altar was there, as was the white path leading to it. Garrett found Celeste sitting in the fourth row on the right, next to the aisle. He took his place in the appreciable gap between her and Michael.

"Good afternoon," Garrett greeted them cheerily. "Beautiful day for a wedding, isn't it?"

"Hello, darling," Celeste glowed. "That shade of blue brings out the color of your eyes."

"Why, thank you, dear. And good afternoon to you, Sir Michael."

Michael crossed his arms. He was wearing black. Garrett followed the boy's glowering gaze to the crucifix—which seemed harmless enough in the light of day.

He couldn't get angry with Michael again, but his light-heartedness ebbed. He looked to the foot of the altar. His rose had either been thrown out or returned to the arrangement. The bloodstain was gone from the carpet. Harold and Candice Warren sat motionless on the front pew.

The audience quieted as the organist transitioned the festive melody into a louder, more somber hymn. Phillip entered from a doorway at right, his expression appropriately serious, and was followed by his best man to the spot where Garrett had stood the night before. The ushers filed by twos down the center aisle, followed by the bridesmaids, and when all were in place before the altar, the music paused. In the silence, the congregated guests stood in unison and turned to face the entrance.

There was some rustling and hesitation in the doorway; then the chords of the wedding march swelled as a stately gentleman started down the aisle with his daughter.

Garrett felt a tug on his sleeve—it was Michael signaling to him. The bride was standing beside Phillip at the altar. Everyone else in the audience was already seated—Garrett released the pew in front of him and joined them. The minister cleared his throat and proceeded:

"Dearly beloved, we are gathered together here in the sight of God, and in the face of this company, to join together this Man and this Woman in holy Matrimony, which is an honorable estate . . ."

As she had walked down the aisle, Garrett had seen the steady pulse beneath the skin of her bare neck; he had seen her naked body pressed against her white lace dress; in her eyes, which had been fixed determinedly ahead, he had seen the reflection of his soul.

". . . and therefore it is not by any to be entered into unadvisedly or lightly, but reverently, discreetly, advisedly, soberly, and in the fear of God. Into this holy estate these two persons present come to be joined . . ."

Garrett's right hand went into his pocket and found the ring that he had purchased for a quarter of his wealth and the Strive Company—no, it had cost him only . . . yes, it had cost him that much. He closed his hand around it and a sharp corner bit into his barely healed wound. With his left hand he took one of Celeste's, grasping it firmly. She smiled—it was the first time he had reached out for her.

"... if any man can show just cause why they should not lawfully be joined together, let him now speak or forever hold his peace."

Moving both hands to the pew in front of him, Garrett stood.

"I can and I do," he said.

She turned and saw him. He gave her a slight nod of greeting—and sat back down.

The warm hush of the cathedral froze to silence, every eye fixed on Garrett, who saw only the bride.

It was she who broke the stillness, turning again to face the altar. The minister cleared his throat nervously—

"Sir, if you would like to explain yourself, please speak up."

But Garrett had nothing more to say.

"Shall we continue?" the minister asked the couple. Phillip didn't seem to understand the question. His bride nodded, and the minister carried on, with a wary eye on Garrett.

"I require and charge you both, as you will answer at the dreadful day of judgment when the secrets of all hearts shall be disclosed, that if either of you know of any impediment why you should not be lawfully joined together in Matrimony, you do now confess it. For be well assured that if any persons are joined together otherwise than as God's Word doth allow, their marriage is not lawful."

Silence.

"Phillip Warren, wilt thou have this Woman to be thy wedded wife, to live together after God's ordinance in the holy estate of matrimony? Wilt thou love her, comfort her, honor and keep her in sickness and in health; and forsaking all others, keep thee only unto her, so long as you both shall live?"

Phillip bent to recover the bouquet that had fallen from his bride's hands, but when he stood to return it, she was no longer there.

There was only the soft brushing sound of the train of her dress as she walked up the aisle and out the door.

The bewildered organist filled the cathedral with the resounding chords of the wedding march. Michael jumped to his feet, applauding.

"Bravo! Good show!" he exclaimed, and turned to Garrett—"Welcome back to the club!"

"Yes . . . Thank you, Michael." Garrett looked at Celeste, who had composed herself perfectly, hands folded in her lap, looking straight ahead as if nothing out of the ordinary had happened. Garrett slipped the ring from his pocket and into Michael's hand.

He whispered in the boy's ear, "Save this for someone you love, Sir Michael. And understand that if you ever give up looking for her, I swear I'll show up at your own wedding and repeat what I said here today."

"I'd rather die," Michael beamed.

"And by the way," Garrett said, while moving to the aisle, "as soon as you're ready, I want you to come to work for me. I could use a good man like you." On seeing the hesitation in the boy's eyes, he added, "Oh—I think you'll approve of a little adjustment to my portfolio that I'll be making in the morning. The details should be in tomorrow evening's business news."

The boy's smile was complete as he watched Garrett stride to the door, where the man's figure became a silhouette against the rectangle of blue summer sky.

She was standing on the curb with her veil in hand, looking across the street to the open field. The breeze played with her auburn hair and sent slow waves across the tall grass.

"Want to go for a walk?" Garrett asked.

"Yes—I do." Her eyes returned his greeting. "It's a beautiful day for a walk."

"If we cut across that field, we can be back in town within an hour."

"Okay."

They crossed the street.

"Where are we going?" she asked.

"Oh, we could stop by a quiet little place I know and have a cup of coffee. They have great food there too, if you would like to have dinner with me later. I hear they'll have a first-rate string quintet playing tonight. How does that sound?"

"Wonderful! I'm hungry already. But let's stop by a store and I'll get something a little more casual to wear. This dress seems a bit too formal for the occasion, don't you think?"

"Of course," he laughed, "but I'm not sure we'll find anything open around here on a Sunday."

"Mine is open," she said, stopping to take off her shoes.

"Yours?"

"Yes, mine—Gratifications."

"Gratifications? . . . But isn't that a national chain?"

"Yes."

"And isn't that chain wholly owned by the Strive Company?"

"Yes, again." She picked a flower and slipped it into her hair.

"But that would mean . . ."

"Yes, it does, and yes, I do."

Garrett took off his own shoes and socks. The grass was cool and the patches of earth warm beneath his feet.

"Good work," he said.

"Thanks."

They jumped a gurgling stream.

"What were you doing at that wedding anyway?" she asked.

He stopped and turned to her. "I'm afraid I was trying to kill you."

She looked up into his eyes and lowered her voice to a soft Italian accent. "Oh, now that is a very serious crime. You should be severely punished. What should I do to you?"

Garrett knew it was a good beginning.

*　　*　　*

*

Holding Your Hand

Knowing that you Are is the joy,
Your voice caresses my mind,
Your smile blesses the earth,
But holding your hand is Knowing,
Knowing that all is well,
    more than well—good,
    more than good—right,
    more than right—
Ours
For the taking, for the loving,
For the joy.

April's Justice

THE POINT OF FOCUS was sixty yards away, four-and-a-half feet above the ground, centered over the wheel ruts of the frozen dirt drive where the drive crested the hill. There was nothing at that point, nothing but the chill, gray December air. The air was held steadily on the tip of a bladed front sight. The blade was couched snugly in a tight "U" notch—the rear sight of a 1903 Springfield .30-06. Inside the rifle's chamber, a small lead ball waited impatiently for a slight contraction of the muscles of the finger on the trigger. On command, the ball would spin madly out of the barrel's biting, spiraling grooves and, within a fifteenth of a second, would hiss across the short distance. Should a man happen to be walking up the drive from the road at that moment, it would be his misfortune to cross the path of the ball—with his chest.

The thought gave her satisfaction, but she didn't smile. Her cheek was pressed hard against the rifle's walnut stock, the occasional snowflake that landed on her face melting there, unnoticed. The cold, oil-cleaned barrel lay steadied across the top of a neat stack of firewood. Over the summer, she had bruised her shoulder again and again as from varying distances she blasted jars and tins to smithereens. The bruises were yellow now; the weapon had become familiar, a constant companion, like the quilted blanket she had carried with her everywhere as a child.

Moments earlier, she had been putting the animals away when she heard an approaching motorcar on the main road. The sound itself would have been acceptable except for its sudden cessation: the farm was the only one along the desolate nine-mile stretch of winding West Virginia road, and no one stopped here, not anymore. She waited behind the firewood, unmoving, watching the tip of the rifle's sight for something to step into the condemned space above the crest of the drive. From the barn behind her, one of the horses snorted restlessly. With her thumb she slipped off the rifle's safety.

A hat appeared, then a head beneath it. Her pulse jumped, and she worked to slow her breathing, steadying her hands, adjusting her aim. She was unprepared for the other two hats, one rising on each side of the drive, outside the ruts. *Okay, first the middle one, then the left, then the right.* The magazine held five rounds—she could afford to miss only twice. She practiced the move, sliding the sight a fraction of an inch each way. *No, it's better just to go straight across—left, middle, right.* She practiced the move twice and held her aim on the place where the chest of the man on the left would appear above the rise within two seconds, and then within one—

A shimmer of silver flashed from the middle man's chest. She recognized the sheriff. The man on the left was Caleb, one of his deputies. She didn't recognize the man on the right, but judging by the hat and badge, he too was a deputy. She practiced the move again—*left, middle, right.*

"April?" the sheriff called out. "April?" he called again, warily.

The trio slowed as they neared. They hadn't spotted her yet. Caleb and the other deputy looked as though they expected ghosts to fly out of the cabin. Twenty yards out, the men stopped, the sheriff observing the wisps of blue smoke rising from the chimney.

"April, this is Sheriff Holsapple. Come on out—I need to talk with you for a minute."

She had never liked the way Deputy Caleb watched her body when she was in town, with that lewd twist sneaking up at the corner of his mouth. She sighted in on the spot and wondered what his face would look like without it. The trigger pressed invitingly against her finger. With the rifle trained on him, she stepped out from behind the woodpile, and the blood drained from the deputies' faces. The three men stood as frozen as the pines behind them.

The sheriff's lips pursed wearily. His shoulders dropped. His hands hung loose and quiet by his sides except for the faint tracing of his right thumb. which seemed to have a mind of its own. If she were going to shoot Caleb first, he might have a chance to draw. She could tell that he wasn't sure if he would or could, that he was thinking that they really shouldn't have come up here, that they should have just left her alone. He was right in thinking that. In the thick stillness, they all knew it.

"Come on now, April," the sheriff ventured. "I'm only here to help."

"I don't need your help, Sheriff."

He sighed. "This is important, April. Look, at least lower the gun. It's too damned cold out here for us all to be sweatin' like this. We'll just stand right here, and you can stand right there, and I'll say my piece and we'll leave, okay?"

She lowered the muzzle of the rifle but kept her eye on Caleb as she turned towards the cabin.

"Please come in, Sheriff," she said. "You must be thirsty."

"Thank you, ma'am."

Caleb exhaled, arching his eyebrows at the other deputy as if to say, "See, I told you she's nuts!" Hesitantly, the two followed the sheriff up the steps of the porch.

Once inside, April leaned the gun against the hearth and, from the kettle on the stove, portioned what remained of the hot apple cider into three cups. The men removed their hats and sat at the sturdy oak table. She served them silently before backing away to the wall, within reach of the gun.

"April, I believe you know Caleb, and this is Tommy Shifflett, my new deputy. Tommy just moved up from Tennessee a few months ago."

Tommy was a handsome, green-eyed young man not much older than April herself. She granted him a curt nod. Caleb received no acknowledgement.

"What's your business, Sheriff?" she asked.

The sheriff set his cup on the table and considered his words carefully.

"Yesterday afternoon, about five miles north of here, a man got away from a Mercer County deputy who was taking him up to the Charleston prison. A posse with dogs searched the hills all night, and today we expanded the search, but he must have holed up somewhere. Now, I doubt you've heard, but there's a blizzard blowing in—"

"I know."

"Well, I expect you would, but anyway, this fella is wearing just regular clothes—no coat, hat or boots—and we figure if he wants to live through the night, he'll likely have to come down out of the storm and find shelter."

"And you think he'll come here?"

"Not necessarily, but here's as good a place as any."

"What did he do, Sheriff?"

He glanced uncomfortably at the deputies. "The man hasn't been convicted yet, but if the charges are serious enough to take him up to Charleston rather than risk the locals lynching him before he can be given a proper trial, then it might be prudent to—"

"Sheriff, what did he do?"

The sheriff sighed, "It doesn't really matter, April—"

"It was murder, wasn't it?"

"Well, yes. Yes, it was murder. . . ."

"And what else?"

He looked around the cabin as though searching for a way out, his eyes pausing momentarily on the closed door to the cabin's only other room. When he looked her in the eye again he grimaced apologetically.

April turned away. Through the window, the snowflakes were bigger now and beginning to fall more thickly. The fire in the fireplace had died down. She laid a handful of kindling on the glowing embers and watched as a small flame leapt to life.

Shoot him, April. Shoot him now!

Caleb chuckled. "The fella's swearin' they've got the wrong man, but don't they all say that? Why, just last month over in Fayetteville, the uncle of that girl who disappeared was claiming that he had only been—"

The sheriff silenced him with a swift, hard look.

April retrieved the rifle.

"Will that be all, Sheriff?"

"Yes, April, that's all. I apologize for the interruption. Thank you for your hospitality. Come on, boys, let's get back to town before the roads get too bad."

The deputies filed out, the sheriff hanging back.

"You know, I've got a daughter your age still at home. I'm sure she would love some company. You're more than welcome to come spend a few days. . . ." He studied her face. "Well, you know where we live if you change your mind. You take care now, April."

Caleb chimed in from the porch. "Miss April, I'd be more than happy to stick around and keep an eye on things for you tonight—"

"—said the fox to the hen," muttered Tommy.

Caleb punched him hard on the shoulder.

"Shut up and walk, both of you," barked the sheriff.

April watched from the porch as the men crossed the yard.

"What's he look like, Sheriff?"

He turned and regarded her, the undersized girl in the oversized coat with the rifle made for war.

"He's a tall fellow with dark hair and light blue eyes. They say you can't forget his eyes. He's wearing a plain white shirt and brown trousers, unless he's stolen some other clothes, and he's got some kind of bird tattooed on his left forearm."

The deputies' hats disappeared first over the crest of the drive, followed by the sheriff's. The car's engine started and faded away into the distance.

The low clouds were coming in dark and fast from the north. The storm was going to be a bad one. The horses had sensed it. Dancer had almost thrown her that morning. She slipped the gun's safety on and went to the barn to put out extra hay and water for the horses and cows, enough to last. In her grandfather's day there had been a blizzard that drifted the snow so deep it had taken him three days to dig from the house to the barn. The new roof she had put on the chicken coop had yet to be tested by the weight of a winter snow: for good measure, she hauled a fence post from behind the barn and wedged it beneath the coop's center beam. After putting out more feed and water for the chickens and pigs, she tied a burlap bag over the well's hand pump and closed up the barn and the sheds. As she was latching the door to the chicken coop, the hens raised such a frantic cackling a person would think they were being buried alive.

There was little to be done for the cabin itself except to secure the shutters. Its sealed logs and thick planks of pine were impregnable to the harsh mountain winters. The doors and windows were tight—there wasn't a single draft. As a child, April had felt completely safe in this house, tucked away in her bed high in the loft, though the storms had howled only a few feet above. She still slept there, on the mattress on the loft's floor, above the bedroom now seldom entered, no longer used, its featherbed shrouded beneath the embroidered white spread, the brush and comb on the vanity untouched, still lying where they had been laid.

From the porch she stood and looked beyond the yard, searching the shifting shadows of the dark and scraggly woods. Dead brown needles carpeted the stands of pine, while those yet on the trees absorbed what winter light they could, their hue a fading memory. The scattered hardwoods stood bare, each lonely and silent amidst its neighbors, limbs naked to the chilling breezes that portended the slashing winds to come.

There was a sharp crack—a branch tumbled from somewhere above, slapping and twisting across the lower limbs until it hit the ground, shattering its brittle fingers.

She reached out to find the porch post, hefting the rifle in her other hand. *Let the storm come. Let the man come.* She was ready.

She went into the house and lowered the iron bar across the door.

After preparing and eating her dinner of squirrel stew, spoon bread and baked apples, she worked on her mending until her fingers tired, then settled into the rocker by the fire to read.

Somewhere in the English countryside, beneath a cascading willow in a flowering spring meadow, a pair of young lovers sat on a blanket plotting their elopement, but it was next to impossible for her to eavesdrop on them for more than a few sentences as the winds had begun to tear at the cabin's eaves and test the shutters' latches. She laid the book aside, pulled her knees up to her chin and wrapped herself in the quilt her grandmother had made. As the minutes and hours ticked away on the clock on the mantel, she rocked, watching the fire.

The wood seemed to be burning more drily and quickly than usual. At this rate, the provision next to the hearth would be depleted by sometime the next morning, and there was less than a quarter of a cord remaining on the porch. After watching the fire awhile longer, she reluctantly extricated herself from her cocoon, donned her coat and boots, lit the lantern, and lifted the bar from the door.

The wind ripped the doorknob from her hand and slammed the door against the wall as a sheet of stinging snow whipped around her and into the house. Slinging the rifle over her shoulder, she pushed her way out, succeeding in pulling the door shut only when the wind slackened momentarily.

There was over a foot of snow on the ground already, and it had drifted twice as high against the side of the cabin. Leaning into the gale, she waded out across the yard, the driving whiteness within the sphere of her lantern's light stinging her eyes. She brushed the accumulation from the top of the wood stack with her coat sleeve, chiding herself for not having thought to move more wood to the porch earlier in the day. One couldn't afford to make such mistakes, living alone in the country. As she struggled to carry a dozen high armloads back to the porch, she found herself angry with the sheriff for having distracted her from her preparations, angry that he had brought Caleb along, angry with Caleb for existing—and for being possum-ugly to boot—angry with herself for allowing herself to be distracted, angry with herself for being angry. From the supplemented supply on the porch, she replenished the stock by the hearth and, using what strength was left in her legs, forced the door closed again. Sinking back against it, she shuddered, thoroughly soaked and chilled to the bone.

Once that she had recovered sufficiently to strip out of her wet clothes and hang them from the mantle to dry, she bundled herself in the quilt and brewed a cup of sassafras tea. With the rocking chair pulled as close to the fire as she could bear, her hair dried quickly, but even after her body was warmed through, the rim of the teacup chattered against her teeth. She picked up her sewing, but her fingers wouldn't hold steady. The wind wailed against the shutters, pressing, tugging, probing unrelentingly. She tried her book again but found her eyes drifting over and over to the beginning of the same paragraph.

There was a thudding bang from somewhere outside—from the direction of the barn perhaps. It could have been anything, a falling branch hitting the chicken coop roof or one of the horses kicking something over. She thought she had heard a whinny. Hopefully, the animals were okay, but she wasn't going back outside, not tonight. It helped to watch the shifting patterns in the coals. The lick of the yellow and orange flames helped warm her soul as the tea warmed her bones. She needed a dog. Maybe in the springtime she could find a puppy. It would need to be a large breed, a good farm dog, maybe a shepherd or a retriever or a hound. A big cuddly mongrel would be fine.

Knock, knock, knock, knock, knock.

The tea spilled over her lap and the cup burst into pieces, scattering across the stone hearth. She froze. She couldn't move.

Oh, my God, I have to move. I must move—now!

She stood, grabbed the rifle and swung it around to the door. She struggled momentarily to keep the quilt from falling away and exposing her body, but the priority for her hands was elsewhere. Raising the rifle to her shoulder, she clicked off the safety as the quilt dropped to the floor.

Good. That's good, April.

Knock, knock, knock, knock, knock.

Her heart plunged—impossibly, the iron bar was leaning against the wall. She had forgotten to put it back after bringing in the wood. There was no other lock on the door. None had ever have been necessary.

Knock, knock, knock, knock, knock.

The shuttered windows precluded anyone from seeing in, but she couldn't see out either. If she ran to bar the door, it would take both of her hands to lift and move the bar—she would have to set the rifle aside to do so. And she wasn't going to do that. There was nothing left but for the doorknob to turn.

Shoot him, April. Shoot him now!

The fear coiled around her vision and tightened until all she could see was the doorknob, with blackness and the accursed memories closing in around it.

It had been a beautiful summer evening in the mountains, the kind of evening that made a person never want to leave. Mama had fixed a scrumptious-smelling venison roast for supper, with fresh vegetables from the garden, and Papa had just come in from his field work. The two were already seated at the table when April dashed in from a swim in the creek. She went straight to the stove and was about to serve herself a plateful of the roast when the man stepped in through the open doorway.

Strangers stopping by wasn't a rare thing that summer. The paper said the country was in a depression, and there were plenty of men out of work. Many of them passed along the road on their way to look for a job in the mines or on their way back from learning that there weren't any jobs to be had. Mama had fed many a hungry man in exchange for his mucking out the stalls, slopping the hogs or some other such chore. Papa wouldn't have minded so much except that Mama never turned away anyone, regardless of any suspected or evident deficiency of character. She didn't check after the men on their assigned work, and not a few had weaseled a meal without lifting a finger. Mama would only shrug and say, "Judge not that ye be not judged."

Knock, knock, knock, knock, knock.

The knocking was more urgent now, the door vibrating with each sound. There was a scratch in the right edge of the doorknob's brass. April watched the scratch intently, waiting for it to move, up or down.

The man who had walked into their house that day had looked about like any other to April, except for the scar through his eyebrow, but her father had seen something more. Unfortunately, her father was seated at the far end of the table, against the wall, in the wrong part of the room to do anything but hope that his daughter would listen to him.

"Get the rifle, April," he had told her, quietly but firmly.

She had reached above the hearth and had taken the rifle from its place. The big bolt-action weapon was the same model her father had carried in the war. He had taught her how it operated, and she had even fired it once though the recoil had knocked her on her back and she hadn't touched it since. She knew enough to slide the bolt rearward and forward again to chamber a round.

"Shoot him, April. Shoot him now!" her father said.

Her mother was beyond shock. "Put that gun down, April Anne! God forgive us! Please don't mind my husband, sir—he was in the war and sometimes—"

The man was walking towards April, watching her intently. She glanced down to make sure the safety was off.

"*Shoot him, April,*" her father ordered. "*You have to do it now!*"

She looked at her mother, then at the approaching man. She raised the rifle and pointed it. Her finger trembled but wouldn't pull the trigger. She started crying. "Papa, I *can't!*"

The man grabbed the rifle from her hands and chuckled. "Should have listened to your old man, young lady." He swept the gun around and shot her father through the chest. "And a woman as saintly and charitable as your dear mother here must be looking forward to meeting her maker too." He shot her and watched her crumple to the floor before turning to April.

"Now, don't you worry, angel—" he took her chin in his hand— "I'm going to take you on a little trip to heaven too, and if you behave yourself, you're gonna live to remember it for a long, long time. And I think I'd like that."

She refused to remember the rest.

Knock, knock, knock, knock, knock.

I'm ready this time, Papa. Oh yes, I'm ready.

She was glad she had left the bar off the door. She wanted to shoot him. She needed it. Her mouth was dry. Why hadn't the scratch moved? How long had he been knocking? She glanced at the clock. It was a quarter after eleven. *All you've got to do is turn the knob, you bastard.*

The gun was heavy, her arms were tiring. Without taking her eye or aim off of the door, she pulled the rocking chair around, rested her foot on the seat and supported her elbow on her knee.

A posse had caught up with the man with the scarred eyebrow three days later. They had hung him on the spot and left him swinging. When April found out, she rode the twenty miles to the place alone and shot five holes through the body. It hadn't helped.

The townspeople attended the burial of her parents beneath the oak in the south meadow. She hadn't told anyone what the man had done to her, but they all knew. She saw it in their eyes and heard it in their voices whenever she had to go into town. The young men were the worst, the way they watched her body, imagining themselves in the man's place.

It was twenty-five after the hour. There had been no knocking in the last ten minutes. Had he gone to the barn to look for a weapon? He could be returning to the cabin with the ax by now. Maybe it wasn't the murderer. But no one in his right mind, probably not even Caleb, would be out in this storm. She dried her palms on her bare leg and waited.

Five minutes more and she could stand it no longer. She dared to lean the rifle against the rocker for just long enough to slip back into her clothes, which were still damp.

"Who is it?" she called, with the rifle aimed again as she approached the door.

There was no reply.

"Who's there?"

Only the wind answered. Taking a deep breath, she reached for the doorknob and, in a single swift motion, turned it, pulled, and leapt back to aim.

The only thing at the door was the storm. She peered out. The snow was freshly scuffled on the porch. Someone had been there, but she could see nothing more through the blowing curtain of white. Hurriedly she slipped on her coat and lit the lantern. He wasn't going to get away this easily, not this time. He was too close to get away. She ventured out into the night, lantern held high, the rifle tucked under her arm.

Though the wind was drifting the snow too fiercely for anything like footprints to survive for long, there remained a faint trail, a shallow trench leading away into the blackness beyond the lantern's light. She followed it in the direction of the barn for several yards and looked behind her. The house was already lost in the darkness and her own steps were quickly being covered. She squinted, blinking against the crystals that were forming on her eyelashes, already regretting not having changed into dry clothes. She had to hurry. A few years ago there was a man in the valley who, in a blizzard not unlike this one, had wandered in circles for hours before dying only twenty feet from his own door. She couldn't see more than two or three feet in front of her or behind.

The tracks veered to the left and seemed to miss the barn altogether, if her sense of direction and distance still served her, but the shallow impressions were becoming indistinguishable in the blowing drifts. She was thinking that she was heading down the hill in the direction of the creek when she tripped over something and fell headlong, dropping the rifle and the lantern as she went down. She knew what the thing was before she hit the ground. Mercifully, the lantern landed upright in a snowbank and stayed lit. She scrambled for the rifle, digging it out of the snow and turning it on the object.

The thing was indeed the body of a man, lying face down. The snow had drifted up over his windward side. She poked at his ribs with the rifle. He didn't move. With the rifle's muzzle, she scraped away some of the snow from his back. He wore no coat. His shirt was white, his trousers brown. She scraped the snow from his left arm and, still employing only the muzzle, pushed up the shirt sleeve. The skin, blanched of most of its color, provided a stark field of contrast to the small, stylishly crafted tattoo of a falcon.

Shoot him, April. Shoot him now!

"Yes, Papa...."

She lowered the muzzle into the curls of dark hair on the back of the man's head. A thought tried to cross her mind, but she forced it away. Laughing aloud, she said to the night—

"This is for Papa, and for Mama, and for *me*."

The freezing trigger felt blood-warm against her finger. The nightmare would now be over. She felt the mechanism's resistance and the familiar give. The same thought tried to surface again but it was easier to ignore the second time around.

But there was a different fear now, a tiny thing struggling to be heard, like the faint cracking in a mine before its collapse. The warning was of something worse than what the other man had done to her, worse than what any man could do—and she was doing it to herself. She sensed the danger, the imminent shredding, crushing and burying of the innermost workings of her mind, a crippling such that it would never work the same for her once the damage had been done. With the pull of the trigger, a part of her soul would die, and she would never be the kind of woman she had always wanted to be, had always aspired to be. She couldn't escape it, she couldn't deny it: if she killed the thought with the man, she might as well then turn the gun on herself. She considered it.

She hated to do it—hated it so much that it made her scream aloud—but with the scream she willed the thought to mind:

He hadn't turned the doorknob.

Not having her consent, this accused murderer and rapist had refused to attempt to enter her home, even though the alternative meant his possibly freezing to death. He hadn't even turned the doorknob. He hadn't turned the knob. . . .

She leaned down and brushed the snow from his face. His eyebrows and eyelashes were encrusted with ice. His cheeks and lips were colorless. She knelt and put her ear to his back. His heart was still beating.

She laid the gun aside and set the lantern in the snow.

It was another late evening on another winter day. April was sitting in the rocking chair by the fire, doing her sewing. Over the years, eight additional rooms had been built around the cabin's original two, but it was the same rocking chair and the same fire. Her granddaughter, Cindy, sat on the sofa next to the rocker, sipping sassafras tea and staring moodily into the embers. Cindy was seventeen now, the second daughter of April's third son.

"What's the matter, honey?" April ventured.

"Nothing, Grandma."

"I'm thinking it's probably something."

Cindy only sighed.

"Boy trouble again?"

Cindy frowned into her tea. "Grandma, there just aren't any good men left out there. Every time I think I've got the right one, he turns out to be something different altogether. If he's not lying to you outright or trying to take advantage of you, he's putting on some kind of a front. You just can't trust them. I hate men."

April smiled to herself. She had been a year younger than Cindy that fateful night, thinner and shorter too. It had taken her over an hour to carry, roll and drag the man to the porch, up the steps and into the house, where she had stripped off his clothes and thawed him by the fire. To stay awake, she had spent the hours until dawn guessing at what his name might be, imagining nearly every one but the right one, as it turned out. It wasn't until early afternoon of the next day that he finally began to stir. As she had waited for him to open his eyes, she was holding the blade of the kitchen knife against his throat, just in case. In her other hand was a cup of hot broth.

"Would you like to hear a story, Cindy?"

Cindy perked up. "Sure, Grandma!"

"Shhh, we must keep our voices down or we'll—"

But it was too late. Grandpa had been snoring softly in his recliner, an open book lying on his chest. His chin had nodded at the sound of their voices. He opened his eyes. Seeing the way his wife was looking at him, he smiled and dozed off again. She had hidden him away for two months, until the crime was confessed by a former farmhand of the victims. And every time he opened those eyes, April fell in love with her Justice all over again.

"Cindy," she asked softly, "have I ever told you the story of how I met your grandpa?"

*   *   *
*

The Line

There was once a line
Crossing the states of Illinois,
Missouri, Nebraska, Colorado, Utah and Nevada.
It was a line of force, a straight line,
Stretched taut between two friends.
When the friends would speak across the line,
It would quiver and contract,
Undulating from the release of tension on both ends.
When the voices were gone,
The wake would lap against the shores of their minds
And the thoughts would begin to build again
Into another unbearable tension,
A satiable need, but barely so,
For there was still that line,
That damned, precious line,
        between them.

The Whistler

IN THE MIDDLE OF THE PLAIN, as though hewn from a mountain of crystalline quartz, rose the city's sun-dazzled facets of towering glass. From the top of the tallest came a sound, a sparkling cascade of notes. The window washers were preparing their scaffolding for the day's descent. One was whistling a symphony. The other two engaged in conversation.

"First day, huh, kid? What's your name again?"

"Bobby. Yours?"

"Walt. So what did you do to deserve this? Parents finally kick you out of the house?"

"No, I'm saving money for school next fall. Besides, I like the view."

"School? Ha. I've got a degree in psychology, and look where it got me."

From the other end of the scaffolding, the whistler nodded a greeting while continuing to check the cables and connections.

"Who's he?" Bobby asked.

"You don't recognize that face?" Walt lowered his voice. "Well, it's been a while, I guess. See that gold-colored building over there?" He tilted his head toward the city's second tallest tower. "He used to sit in a plush corner office on the top floor. That man was once the president of his own bank—and now he's washing the windows on one. He's the biggest failure this side of the Mississippi."

"Damn."

As the platform lowered over the edge, the symphony segued into a melody that had once serenaded cattle on the rolling prairie below, the notes lofting into blue space.

"So, what happened to him?" Bobby asked.

"He made a bad decision, ran into some bad luck. The bank went under."

"Oh."

Three floors lower, a mockingbird landed on the platform's railing. It cocked its head at a Viennese waltz and flew off in search of less formidable competition.

"Why didn't he start over or go into some other line of business?"

"With what? Every penny he had was backing that bank. His credit is shot. Up there on the north side, he had a twenty-room mansion, four cars, a yacht, a summer home in the mountains. Now he rents a room down near that factory by the rail yard; he walks to work, doesn't have so much as a bathtub to play in, and he hasn't taken a day's vacation in the two years he's worked here."

The waltz shifted into a lilting ragtime tune, the first of a dozen that carried them down the next seven floors.

"Does he have family?"

"His wife took the kids. The relatives who once basked in his glow now cross the street to avoid his shadow. One of his brothers even changed his last name."

A series of Baroque canons and fugues accompanied them down to the building's halfway point, where they paused for lunch. After eating his sandwich and tucking away the brown bag, the biggest failure this side of the Mississippi laid back on the platform to watch the clouds, whistling a soulful slave hymn.

"Surely he still has a friend or two," Bobby ventured. "If the decision was just an honest mistake and the circumstances were unforeseeable, he would still have the respect of his peers. Somebody would give him a chance at something. . . ."

"People want him around like they want a black cat named Thirteen. If whoever is in charge of this place ever bothered to read the applications for window washer and discovered that bad luck incarnate is hanging on the side of their bank, they'd probably cut the cables we're dangling from rather than waiting for us to come down."

As the afternoon passed, a lively march reverberated from the surrounding buildings, followed by an operatic aria and a program of buoyant show tunes. The sidewalks began filling with people on their way home. A sweet lullaby floated down. A few glanced up appreciatively.

"Well, at least he seems happy," Bobby said.

"At first I thought he'd taken this job just to have a convenient place to jump from, but then he started with that infernal whistling and I knew he'd lost his mind. The only future the man has is the hope of being back up on top of this godforsaken pile of glass tomorrow morning."

An Irish ballad set them gently on the sidewalk.

"Hey, you—the whistler." A man in a business suit beckoned from a bench next to the taxi stand.

"Here, this is for the music," he said, holding out a five-dollar bill and patting the spot beside him. "Sit down, sit down. . . . Nobody whistles like that anymore, you know. My father was a whistler though. God, could he whistle. When I asked him to teach me how, he said, 'Son, you have to start with a clean conscience.' It took me a long time to understand that, but he was right. He was the most indomitable man I've ever known. I'll never forget, when I was seven years old a tornado destroyed our house and the farm. My father led us up from the cellar, took a long look around, and as he tossed a twisted piece of our plow aside, he started whistling. I only remember a little of the tune. It went—*La, dah dee dee, la dah, dah dee la . . .*"

The whistler's whistle picked up the melody and carried it high into the glass canyon.

"Yes! . . . Yes, that's it. . . ."

The next morning, on the top floor, there were only the two window washers cleaning the panes.

Walt exclaimed, "Come here, kid, look at this!" His face was plastered to the glass. "Now I know what happened to him—he got himself fired. That man, the one he was talking to, he's the bank president!"

Bobby went and looked, and returned to his own side in a thoughtful melancholy. He wiped a swath through the dust on a window and stopped, peering into the office next to the president's. The well-dressed man sitting at the desk was cleaning a smudge off of the glass top with his handkerchief. On the front of the office door, someone was lettering a name in the space above the words, "Vice President." The only sound outside was the wind, but the man at the desk was undoubtedly whistling. Recognizing Bobby, he waved. Bobby waved back and finished cleaning the window.

As the scaffolding lowered to the next floor, Bobby shaped his mouth in the form of an "O"—and blew.

*   *   *
*

Your Hands

Your hands move
    and the Earth takes form.
Your eyes call Life
    from the clay.
With a mother's love
    you bring children to bear.
From your lips
    comes the breath of their souls.

You straighten the shoulders
    and lift the chin,
Smooth the brow with a finger,
    caress the cheek,
Brush back the hair
    and lighten the eye,
Take them out
    to be seen by the world—

In my heart
    they fill the place
    you created.

The Seduction of Santi Banesh

HER EYES FLUTTERED OPEN. The plane's cabin was still dark and most of the passengers were still sleeping though a band of pink had broken the cold blues to the east. She had napped only fitfully on the transpacific flight. Across the aisle, the graying man in the crumpled business suit who had been staring at her through most of the night was now snoring, his head back and mouth open. In the row ahead of him the handsome god in tennis shorts was reading a paperback, his exposed leg smooth and firm, the skin deeply tanned. Her finger moved along the armrest of her seat, unconsciously tracing the groove between his muscles, from beneath the tennis shorts, down the length of the thigh, rising gently to the knee, cutting in again down the calf to the ankle. Below the short sleeve of his shirt, his well-defined arm flowed to long, strong fingers, which stroked her hair gently as her open lips sought the most succulent part of the thigh, halfway between—

Her hand whipped from the armrest to clutch the amulet hanging between her breasts. Her parents were still sitting quietly in the row ahead of her. Beside her, her little brother, bless his heart, had his face plastered to the window, watching the sea below. Through her robe she held the amulet tightly and closed her eyes. She hadn't eaten in three days, and there were still five days to go. She tried not to think of it. One day at a time, she reminded herself. One hour at a time. She had to compose herself, to be strong, to fight her body. And how was it that men were looking more and more like food?

Santi Banesh was a sultan's dream of dark olive skin and burnt-umber eyes, deep almond pools that could drown a man. The long loose folds of her traditional wrap tried to hide her body, but her enchanting eyes, slender hands, the rise and fall of her chest and her graceful, sensual walk only made the robe work contrary to its intention, its overt defenses posing a rude challenge to imaginations which proceeded to lay waste to its veiling walls. Imaginations can be thorough beasts: Santi had already been ravaged by hundreds of men, though she was still a virgin and only fifteen.

And now, just as her body was straining for perfection, it was starving. A third day without food and it was screaming. Everyone had said that after two days the hunger pangs abated, and for most girls they probably did, but her insides had set up a protest which started about an hour before the first missed meal and had only escalated since. She had always been a healthy eater anyway. Her mother scolded that she would turn into an elephant once she bore children. But Santi's body burned more brightly and hotly than most—it needed the food—and it found this deprivation unforgivable.

She would rather have been severely beaten than be the cause of her own torture, but she knew that this was exactly the point of the ritual anyway: the eight-day Fast of Virgins was to teach control of physical desire and conquest of the hungry body. It was the highest duty and honor of every girl in the spring of her fifteenth year, at the critical age when a girl knew what it was to want, but hopefully before she had done anything about it. The wisdom of ancient clerics had shown that if a woman learned to starve herself of food, there was a much better chance, though not a guarantee, that she would be able to resist sexual temptation as well.

Santi had worn the customary amulet, which hung from a silver chain around her neck, since she was thirteen. It was engraved with the figure of a kneeling woman. If once caught cheating during the Fast of Virgins, she would lose the amulet. No amulet—no husband, and she would spend her life tending her parents' home. And if she were caught so much as kissing a man before marriage, she would be publicly stoned by her community leaders, family and friends. Santi wanted to be good—she really did—but she had determined in advance that if she were ever to be stoned, she would get a hell of a lot more than a kiss for her troubles. The thought of men made her stomach growl again, and taking a last look at the tennis shorts, she tried to banish both hungers from her mind.

Her little brother was eating honey-roasted peanuts. When he saw his sister's eyes fasten on the bag, he made a quick check of their parents and silently pushed the peanuts toward her. Santi gently pushed them back and kissed him on the forehead. Andjani was eight years old and even more beautiful than she, with the same dark features, rich skin tone and quiet grace. Girls openly envied his eyelashes. He would often come to his sister's room at night and crawl into bed with her.

The parents, Rakeel and Sumi Banesh, were model citizens. Rakeel was Vice Minister of Foreign Affairs, and his wife was the Wife of the Vice Minister of Foreign Affairs. They moved in the highest of their respective circles and were well regarded. The children had been expected of them and were a fine touch when entertaining in their modestly luxurious home, which had both electricity and indoor plumbing.

Their nation was at least equivalent in size to an average Texas ranch, and its theocracy was respected and feared by neighboring countries, though few others were aware of its existence. Up until now Rakeel's job of assisting with foreign affairs had been relatively simple, due to the general lack thereof, but his superior had been bedridden with malaria only three days before a critical appointment with a reviewing committee of the World Bank—and now the task had fallen to Rakeel. He was excited and equally nervous: a successful wooing of the World Bank meant instant acclaim and an assured promotion, but if he said anything stupid enough to cause a decrease in the current funding level, he would surely go the way of a former colleague who had committed that very sin a few years ago. There was a saying in the language similar to the English "sink or swim," but it was used more literally, and the "swim" wasn't really an option.

The meeting was scheduled for 10 a.m. the next day in New York City, but first they were flying into San Francisco, where today he was to meet with board members of a local museum concerning a future display of his country's "primitive art." He was certain he could supply the stuff in ample quantity, even if it had to be created specially for the occasion. The exhibit could be a great boon to his country's tourism.

The family was along only because the Minister of Internal Security had hinted that he wouldn't mind watching their house while they were absent, which meant that he wanted to use it for an illicit tryst. The thought of the man's fat, oily body rolling around in his bed nearly made Rakeel sick, but the position of Minister of Internal Security had certain fringe benefits, such as being able to murder at will. Rakeel made a mental note to buy a new set of sheets while in the States—the good soft ones that you couldn't get back home.

The plane had descended through a drizzling fog to the level of the surrounding hilltops, and the waters of the San Francisco Bay were coming up fast beneath the craft's belly. Rakeel closed his eyes in fretful anticipation of the inevitable jolt of the landing. A full thirty seconds after it should have happened his eyes popped open in terror—but the pilot was already taxiing slowly toward the terminal. The passengers hadn't felt a thing. *Damn these cocky Americans with their we-can-do-everything-perfectly attitudes*, he thought. *One of these days they'll be brought to their knees. . . .*

The plane rolled to a stop, and a flurry of activity converged on them through the wetness—yellow towing vehicles, fueling trucks, cargo escalators, elevating food-and-beverage trucks and white tractors pulling trains of luggage cars. As Santi watched the well-oiled precision of the rain-suited men and their clean machines, there was an uneasy, excited stirring within her. It was like one of the hunger pangs, but deeper. There was something very different about this place. Her breathing quickened and she reached for Andjani's hand. The lights on a massive jet beside them winked as it was pushed away from the terminal, toward the runway.

The limousine door shut, and at last, they were safe. None of them had spoken a word since they had left customs and started walking through the terminal.

The assault on their senses had actually begun when they first boarded the jet aircraft nine hours earlier, but by the time they landed they had become somewhat accustomed to the friendly smiles, the cushioning comforts, the little technologies of the cabin, and the beautifully, colorfully dressed people. Santi had decided that, when airborne, people just didn't seem to weigh as much.

Rakeel had expected a jolt when landing, but if the plane had done a half roll and landed on its back, it would have been less of a shock than the one he received in the terminal. There was no military band, no cluster of greeting potentates, no perfunctory crowd of cheering citizens. Soft piano jazz floated down from unseen speakers. The uniformed man he mistook for the mayor only nodded, put their luggage on a cart and walked away with it. The few people who bothered looking their way only smiled, either quizzically or warmly.

They had hurriedly followed the skycap. The terminal was equally unfathomable to Sumi and the children. There was no rude shoving and scuffling, no machine guns, no livestock. The place was bright, shining and clean, though they saw no one cleaning it. Lights, chrome, glass and steel—everything looked new. There were shops and stands packed with the most beautiful clothes, magazines and books, stuffed animals, flowers, gold-foiled boxes of candies, and trinkets of every sort. There were barbershops and shoeshine stands. Escalators, elevators, and moving walkways which Sumi refused to step onto. Bars, cafes and restaurants that opened right out into the terminal proper. Not a single dirty beggar to avoid. Andjani didn't let go of his sister's hand, but his eyes were those of a pirate who had espied a Spanish galleon riding fat and heavy with gold bullion. Santi couldn't stop watching the faces of the people. How could they be so . . . so . . . ?

By the time the family had followed their luggage through the automated sliding glass door to the outside, Rakeel was furious, Sumi was terrified, and the children were simply in shock.

"Welcome to America!" the limo driver beamed. Lalek was a fellow countryman who had come to the States six years ago to attend college and now made his living driving between the airport and the city. He had already made enough money to buy the sleek, black limousine he was driving, and he expected to finance a second car within the year. Soon, he would be running a small fleet. That his motherland could still track him down had somewhat concerned him, but the prospect of playing tour guide to someone from his own country, and a high government official no less, had been irresistible. The three additional family members were entirely unexpected, and the sight of the lovely girl from home unsettled Lalek nearly as much as her new surroundings had affected her. He straightened his cap and became the world's best chauffeur, insisting that they not raise a finger to assist with the luggage or open their own doors. The enthusiasm only further irritated Rakeel, who ordinarily thrived on such servility—he wanted it from an American.

Santi thought the young man charming in his cap, jacket and bow tie. The car was splendid, more luxurious than anything at home, and he would be chauffeuring her around like a princess. When he asked if she would like her handbag put in the trunk with the rest of the luggage, she knew he expected no such thing. His tone and penetrating stare were suggesting something else entirely, and she didn't entirely mind.

The limo whisked them from the airport and into the traffic of the ten-lane freeway heading north, Lalek swiftly maneuvering into the center lane. Rakeel whispered to his wife that she looked foolish clinging to the door handle. She folded her hands rigidly in her lap.

The sun had burned off the morning fog, and the traffic was drying the road. Andjani had already decided that someday he would have a red car without a roof, with a white leather interior, just like the one in the far left lane with the silver emblem on its hood that looked like a three-pronged steering wheel. The driver was a young woman in sunglasses. As the car passed, Santi marveled at the blond hair flying in the wind.

Lalek, ogling the blonde until she was out of sight, nearly side-swiped a truck beside them.

"It's a decadent country, Minister Banesh, and it's going down-hill fast, the way of Rome, India, England, Spain, France—all of the once-great empires. Pride, greed and lasciviousness bring them all down in the end. Far better to be an obedient and humble people such as we." He glanced at Santi through the rearview mirror. She turned away to watch the cars.

The freeway was a gleaming metal rainbow of color, and it was going somewhere, the same somewhere she was going. But the drivers, they all knew what was ahead. Their determined faces both excited and frightened her. She looked around, feeling as if she were being swept along in the middle of a river by a mile-a-minute current. There could be no stopping. The hunger was making her dizzy and weak, and her fingers went again to the amulet. Her feet reached for something, anything against which to brace herself, but there was nothing within reach in the back of the black limousine. She closed her eyes and leaned her head back against the leather, wondering how Lalek would look naked.

Andjani tugged at her sleeve. They were rounding a turn in the freeway, cresting the top of a hill, and there before them lay the city, sweeping from west to east, across the hills and down to the bay. The vast, intricate spread of interconnected pinnacles, domes, parapets, grand halls and gardens was nothing less than a modern fairytale palace. Tufts of fog clung to the edge of the bay beneath a double-decked bridge which arched out and over to an island of green, only to leap away again into the eastern haze. The sunlight had gathered on a greenhouse roof atop a slender hilltop apartment tower, from where it was scattered in a sunburst through the lingering morning mists. The vision was wrapped in ribbons and bows of highway, one end of which swept out to them to flow beneath the wheels of the car. Santi laughed aloud.

Her father glared at her and her mother stared as if, right before their eyes, their daughter had turned into a toad. Rakeel apologized to Lalek and, to Santi's chagrin, revealed that she was in the third day of the Fast, implying that she wasn't to be held entirely accountable for her state of mind.

"Well, you've picked the perfect time to visit San Francisco then. Did you know that this city has more restaurants per capita than any other in America? These people are slaves to their stomachs. It's nothing but a sprawling brothel of materialism and carnality. Your daughter will be the purest of the pure—a mountain shrine should be built to her—once she withstands the temptations of—" he couldn't possibly have thought it—"of the many restaurants here. . . ." But he had thought it, the course of action having arrived complete in his mind. Yes, there were far more tempting things in this sinful city than its eating establishments—and there was the other way, the better way, to break the Fast of Virgins. His eyes dimmed in anticipation. Ripe figs were meant to be eaten.

The city grew around her, first softly tugging, then sweeping her forward, drawing her in with a steady, incessant offering of sights and sounds. She was descending into its gray, pulsing veins, being pulled inexorably into its core.

At a hotel near Union Square, they stopped and left their luggage in a room. After a moment of freshening up, Rakeel took a taxi to his meeting, and the others were back in the limousine before Santi had time to catch her breath.

It was nearly noon. They drove down to Fisherman's Wharf and Pier 39, where Sumi and Andjani ate lunch while Santi wandered in and out of the cornucopia of shops, Lalek following at a discreet distance. The wealth of colorful clothing enveloped and cradled her. The gleaming, sparkling jewelry was laid out and waiting. In the middle of a shop of stuffed animals, she turned in a slow circle, imagining it was her bedroom. She touched her nose to the nose of a life-sized gorilla and whispered baby talk in the ear of a teddy bear while holding it to her cheek. In middle of the pier she stood and watched the people who had come from every corner of the planet. One couldn't distinguish by race or by dress the residents of the city from the tourists, but the tourists all carried a disoriented look about them, and the people of the city looked—at home. Yes, that was it.

She'd never seen quite that look before, not even in her own country. Especially there. These people belonged here, on this earth, in this country, in this city. And it belonged to them.

She walked with Lalek back to the restaurant where they had left Sumi and Andjani. The smell of freshly baked sourdough bread and hot clam chowder tried to fill the vacuum in her body. From the open window of a candy shop, a thick, sweet odor of rich chocolate reached out, and the sidewalk nearly slipped from under her feet.

In the limousine again, they drove south to the shipyards and walked along a dock between the looming cold grays of a destroyer and a battleship. Above, raised rows of massive guns promised to protect, with pitiless raw power. Andjani reached out to try to touch the side of the destroyer and nearly fell in the bay, causing his mother to shriek.

They parked beneath the Embarcadero Center, where in an arcade the children stopped to play a virtual-reality gunfighter game. The shops here were a step up from those on the more touristy pier. This was where the people working in the towers above spent their salaries. The place smelled of money—selective money. Santi's fingers caressed the crystal bottles of magical liquid on a perfume counter. A salesgirl sprayed a breath of deliciously erotic scent on her arm, and Santi twirled around, imagining herself wearing the bright-blue party dress being modeled for her by an aloof mannequin. She couldn't fathom the quantities, the rack-after-rack, row-after-row quantities of variety and styles. She found three stores that sold only shoes. Imagine, only shoes.

Sumi spent all of her time trying to reel in her children, first Andjani, then Santi, and once she found Santi, Andjani would be gone again. The place was full of seductive demons—Sumi could feel it— and she openly frowned upon the whores behind the sales counters with their bare arms, painted faces and uncovered heads. She felt terribly homesick and couldn't wait until the trip was over. The best she could do for now was to protect the children as well as she was able.

The next stop was Coit Tower, where they climbed to the top to look out over the city and watch a fleet of yachts racing past Alcatraz

Island. Then it was on to the Golden Gate Bridge, which they crossed and re-crossed before circling beneath to Fort Point. As the afternoon breeze kicked up the waves against the rocks, Santi marveled at the bridge's naked red-orange skeleton towering above, a pencil-drawn equation of triangles and arches. Then it was back into the city, and up three blocks of the steepest grade imaginable, the limo's engine laboring and whining. The cars that were parked straight into the curb looked as if they were about to topple and roll down the hill. At the top of the climb, Lalek turned the car, traveled one block and turned back down a street that was even steeper than the one they had come up, on the flat intersections accelerating to give his passengers a moment of weightlessness as the car's nose dove down the next block. Sumi was in such a state that she didn't realize that her son was insisting the cycle be repeated, until they had climbed again and were on their way back down. Santi laughed like a girl on a swing.

Golden Gate Park soothed with its cool forests, smoothly stretched lawns and geometrical gardens. There was no time for the museums, but she begged to stop at the merry-go-round, where she rode a fierce dragon while Andjani shot at Indians from atop his trusty steed. At a vendor's stand nearby, Lalek bought a Coke and a large soft pretzel with mustard on it for Andjani. Santi turned away. She watched a handsome young father walk by with triplet boys in tow, all dressed in identical designer clothes.

They drove west to the ocean, past the Cliff House, then south along the beach and over Devil's Slide, a potential avalanche threatening from the cliffs above on the left and a long plunge to the ocean on the right. Then it was back into the city, past the zoo and through the Haight, where the storefronts were decorated in black, blue and voodoo and the inhabitants paraded a bohemian sideshow of tattoos, hair art and piercings. One young woman stuck out her tongue to a friend to show off six rings skewered through it. Sumi swore a mortified curse under her breath, and the children squealed their language's equivalent of "Gross!" while Lalek laughed and laughed.

They stopped to window-shop in Union Square, the terraced block of landscaped public space which was surrounded by some of the most luxurious and expensive stores on the coast. Just as Santi had calculated that the price of the feminine black business suit in a display window would cost three months of her father's salary, and would be quite impossible for anyone to buy, a woman walked out of the store wearing the very thing. Andjani was spellbound as he examined the wonders of a three-story toy store—a Spanish galleon was a pitiful comparison.

On the square, Santi noticed a curious grouping of people whose attention seemed focused around someone in their midst, like worker bees buzzing around their queen. She crossed the street to get a closer look. It was a high-fashion model going through her paces on a photo shoot, with only the city as her backdrop. She was the most confident, beautiful and happy person Santi had ever seen. The woman turned and strode toward the camera, then turned and walked away again. She stopped in the middle of the square and raised her eyes to the tops of the buildings. The next exposures were burned for eternity on the screen of Santi's memory, and she knew in that moment that, someday, she too would be a model. On one heel, with uplifted arms and outstretched fingers, the woman spun all the way around, touching the whole of San Francisco. Santi had seen the look in the eyes only once before—through a neighbor's bedroom window.

Andjani dragged them into a sporting goods store and determined that what he wanted was an oversized San Francisco Giants sweatshirt and a pair of heavily padded, high-top Nike basketball shoes. He had smuggled his entire savings, a considerable sum, into the country with him and, unbeknownst to his mother, had at some point during the day persuaded Lalek to trade him the equivalent in U.S. dollars. He was already trying on the shoes, and Santi couldn't help but giggle over how huge they looked stuck on the ends of his little legs. But Andjani wanted both the shoes and the sweatshirt. He marched proudly to the counter with his prizes. It was then that his mother realized that he actually had money, and once she had discovered that it was his own, she refused to allow him to spend it on such frivolities, which he couldn't possibly wear at home anyway. They would have cost nearly every cent he had. Andjani's bottom lip quivered and his eyes glistened, but he swallowed the tears, lifted his chin and carefully, neatly, replaced the merchandise on the shelf. He followed his mother out of the store like an innocent man being led to the gallows. For the remainder of the afternoon, he was lost in an eight-year-old's thoughtful melancholy.

They were driving again when Lalek turned left through an oriental arch, a veritable space warp that deposited them 8,000 miles to the west, in the city's Chinatown. In an intersection eight blocks farther, they skipped another hemisphere and landed in the Italy of North Beach. Lalek was keeping a close eye on Santi, who was saying less and less and blinking more and more, her saturated mind struggling to stay focused as the afternoon pounded on. His well-planned route and timing were working perfectly. It was now five o'clock. He had to have them back at the hotel by six-thirty, when they would pick up Rakeel and go straight to the airport to catch the flight to New York.

He parked the car in front of a particular Italian restaurant and herded Sumi and Andjani inside for an early dinner, slipping the maitre d' a twenty and telling him to make sure the service was slow. He walked away with Santi, and just before the next street corner, he stopped and turned to her.

"Now I'm going to show you something that maybe no other girl from our country has ever had the chance to see. I'm taking a big risk by doing this—I know you'll never tell your parents—but I really like you and I thought you deserved to see it. You've experienced only the thin surface of this city. Do you want to see what's below? What lies at its heart?"

She nodded, her pulse quickening, as a bundle of heavy clouds slid in front of the sun.

He led her around the corner. The street was lined on both sides with garish signs, their neon lights flashing palely. Many of the bulbs framing the marquees were burnt out. Even the best-kept buildings had a drab, used look to them. A finely sculpted neon figure of exaggerated feminine curves was lit in red, and many similar representations were painted on signs and walls next to dark openings and heavily curtained doorways. Most of the women pictured were wearing little or no clothing; their faces held something in common with the faces of the women standing in the doorways. The men in the area had something of the same look. It was if they all shared the same, unspoken secret, though none of them seemed terribly happy about it.

There were few windows along the street. The existing ones displayed rubber and plastic body parts of unusual sizes. Santi thought that perhaps these were prostheses. The various apparatus displayed held no meaning for her.

A light drizzle had begun to fall. Lalek stopped in front of one of the nicer facades and spoke to the girl at the door as though he knew her. The girl's eyes travelled over Santi's body the way a man's would, and she nodded approvingly. As Santi followed Lalek through the door, she felt the girl's eyes trying to catch her own.

Inside, Lalek paid a man at a window, then paid him some more and the man gave him a key. Lalek took Santi's hand and led her through the foyer. He pushed aside a crimson velvet curtain.

They were in a small theater lit only by two naked red bulbs, one on each side of a wooden stage. The stage floor appeared to have stains on it, and it was empty save for a single wooden chair in the center. Facing the stage were a dozen rows of red theater seats, the fabric frayed, stained and pocked with cigarette burns. Six solitary figures were already seated haphazardly about the room, waiting. As Lalek led her to the middle of the back row, one of the nearer men, his jaw slack, stared at her body, undeterred by the presence of her companion. He reminded her of an uncle who had displayed his privates to her when she was seven years old. The air was heavy, moist, and uncomfortably silent. The room smelled of scented disinfectant. She fingered her amulet nervously. Lalek checked his watch.

Finally, from the speakers below the red lights came a low, deep rhythmic booming. She could feel the vibration in her chest. Lalek leaned over and put his hand on her arm.

"Are you afraid? Do you want to leave?"

She was afraid, but she shook her head. She was going to find out what happened on that stage. His hand remained on her arm.

The red lights went out, and for a moment the theater was pitch black. Then the chair appeared in a hot yellow spotlight, and the rest of the stage was lit in dim blue. Four solitary figures glided out, one from each of the shadowed corners. They began to step to the steady rhythm, moving clockwise around the edges of the stage. There were two men and two women, each in a white robe, each barefoot. On the next round, they were closer to the chair, watching each other, and so it proceeded, the circle tightening on each turn. When they reached the edge of the spotlight, they spread their arms and held hands. After another full turn, the rhythm stopped, and so did the circle.

The room was silent. Santi could hear her heartbeat. She tried to slow her breathing. The rhythm returned, a little louder, a little faster, joined by the metered chanting of deep male and high female voices. In time with the beat, three of the participants closed around the fourth—one of the women—and they lifted her above their heads. They turned her slowly above the chair, then lowered her into it. Their hands began to move over her body. Santi felt a flush rise to her face. The rhythm and chanting were subtly rising and quickening. The woman's robe was carefully removed to reveal her nakedness, and the hands continued to work. Then the hands were joined by mouths.

Santi's cheeks burned. Her palms were wet. The woman in the chair was replaced by one of the men, and the rhythm built. The first woman remained naked and became the central participant in the man's treatment.

The second woman was seated. Then the second man. The rhythm pounded Santi's eyes. The sense of structure on the stage was blurring as identities were lost. A hand was stroking a thigh—she could feel on her own body its pressure and heat. She glanced down to find Lalek's hand on her leg, mirroring the motion, working its way higher. She focused on the stage again. From the intertwined bodies she made out the faces. The expression on one was completely blank; two shared the secret of those outside; the fourth was twisted in hatred.

She took Lalek's hand from her leg, held it and nodded toward the exit. He rose eagerly and led her through the curtain, turning away from the front door to lead her toward a flight of stairs, digging for the room key in his pocket. At the foot of the stairs she stopped and pulled him into the shadows below the staircase. She put her arms around his neck and studied his eyes. As he reached greedily for her breasts, she kneed him so hard in the groin that when he dropped to the floor, he didn't move or make a sound.

She nodded politely to the man behind the window and ignored the girl at the door. Outside, it was still raining lightly. When she reached the corner, she stopped and turned. No, she thought, this isn't the heart of the city. It isn't even a characteristic feature. And from that moment forward she chose to ignore it.

Rather than turning toward the restaurant, she crossed the street and kept walking, letting the rain wash away the memory. She was faint from hunger, but the sounds of the traffic and the solid concrete beneath her feet reassured her. Her mind traveled again over the course of the day. The city had startled her with its beauty and strength. It had sweetly offered a sultan's wealth of the finest things, with a promise to protect and the prospect of a lifetime of exciting tomorrows. Its hard angles, firm curves and towering planes weighed upon her gently. Its sea-touched air kissed her forehead. As the sun shone through the last of the showers, she reached for her amulet, though she could no longer remember why.

At the next corner she turned and stopped. She was standing in the city's most powerful artery, filled with rush-hour traffic. On both sides, the ever-heightening stairways of steel and glass were rising and tapering to dominate the sky. As her eyes were pulled upwards, her head lifted, and as the lines of the buildings thrust her gaze heavenward, her body at last surrendered to the city's pleasure. There, in the middle of a crowd of hurrying pedestrians, she collapsed to the pavement.

The circle of concerned faces hovering above her registered relief and then wonder—the girl was even more beautiful when she opened her eyes. They helped her to her feet, though she hardly needed it. She felt weightless, at perfect peace—and hungry.

There was a hotdog cart on the corner. She had no American money but extended an offering of what she had. The vendor's reluctance to accept the meager palmful of strange coins melted before a look of longing and anticipation the likes of which he hadn't seen since leaving his own country. With a smile usually reserved for his daughters, he watched as Santi loaded her acquisition with every condiment available and washed it down with a diet soda. With the balance of her funds, she repeated the process, and in sated contentment, she walked back to the restaurant.

Sumi and Andjani were standing at the curb, looking perplexedly at the vacant space where the limousine had been. Santi managed with sign language to have the maitre d' call a taxi for them.

It was six forty-five when they returned to the hotel—fifteen minutes late for departing to the airport. Rakeel was in a lather as they frantically gathered their luggage from the room. In the lobby, Sumi glanced around to discover that Andjani had wandered off again. One parent hurried in one direction and the other in the opposite to search for him. Santi silently thanked her little brother for unerringly coming to her aid this one last time. Missing him would be the worst of it.

Picking up the smallest of her bags, which in the room she had hastily repacked with a few necessities and a change of clothes, she walked out of the door and down the street.

At first she had no particular destination. She needed only to put distance between herself and the hotel. They would never find her. Her father would catch the flight to New York regardless, with or without her, and her mother would dutifully follow. Santi was free, and as the city began to turn on its lights, she felt an immense gratitude to every person, every brick, and every inch of the evening sky.

Several blocks farther, she stopped and turned, having the feeling that she was being followed—but she recognized no one. Picking up her pace, she made several erratic turns, cutting through a department store and then a parking garage. The feeling remained with her, but she was less afraid of it.

She knew her destination now. She was angling her way back to the heart of the financial district. The street corner where she had collapsed, which had been filled with pedestrians only a short time before, was now empty. Thin columns of lighted rectangles climbed the office buildings. She took the amulet from beneath her robe and unlatched the chain. Kneeling, she kissed it, then pushed it down into a crack in the pavement.

She needed somewhere to spend the night. Tomorrow would be a busy day, the first of her modeling career. She had no more money. She looked around. There was a shadowed niche in the side of an office building, where warm air flowed from a grating at the bottom of the wall. This would do nicely. She made herself as comfortable as she could, resting her head on her bag, and instantly fell asleep beneath the city's protective gaze. She didn't even fully awaken when the little boy in an oversized Giants sweatshirt and Nike basketball shoes snuggled into her arms.

*   *   *
*

Priceless

There is demon in my angel,
    but not enough to damn.
With caresses comes a knifing,
    and a kiss upon the wound.
Her diamonds are sharp-edged,
    dazzling while they cut.
A sip of glass-laced wine,
    my scarlet communion flows.

There is hell within my heaven,
    yet it's heaven all the same.
Only look upon me, Angel,
    let me see it once again,
And again I'll empty my coffers
    for that precious,
    priceless
smile.

In My World

There's a place I can go in the doldrums of day,
    when life's burdens weigh heavy upon me.
There's someone beside me in the dark chill of night,
    when alone, I reach out for heat.
There's a soul I can turn to when no one is there,
    when no other on earth resonates.
There's a body that fills me when I'm starving for joy,
    when I can't recall why I am here.

There is you,
    and all is right
In my world.

For the Woman
Who Has Everything

SARAH WOKE TO SILENCE. Thin lines of moonlight lay in
diagonals across the floor. She listened for awhile. The only sound
was the soft rustle of her hair against the pillow.

She slid her legs from beneath the layers of blankets and let her
feet touch the chill of the hardwood floor. As she walked, a line of
moonlight slipped around one ankle, then the other, ascending,
scanning and measuring her body in strict undulations. At the west
window the moon caught her fully, a slender white animal beneath the
new winter's sky.

To the north the terraced lawns twinkled with frost as from a
sprinkling of ground glass. To the south the meadow's tall grasses
were broken, the stalks strewn like fallen soldiers, the stumps standing
like nails on the hills. Below and before her lay the expansive gardens,
where the moonlight was caught in webs of shadow beneath the bare
rose bushes and in chains of diamonds beneath the arched trellises.
Beyond the gardens the shadows converged in venous networks that
covered the forest floor and stretched down to the lake. The black
water held a solitary, struggling prisoner, the twin sister of a star
above. Beyond the circle of the horizon lay the borders of the estate.
Within, the only movement, the only sound, the only life was the faint
beating of Sarah's heart.

She wrapped herself in her robe and stepped into her slippers.
The bed hardly looked slept in. In the long hall, the moonlight floated
in slanting shafts from the skylights to oblique rectangles on the wall.
It was still her habit to pause at each of the children's rooms. In Kelly's,

the moonlight glinted from a fleet-footed Mercury atop one of the running trophies. The stuffed animals waited patiently on the bed. Kelly was doing well in law school, her holiday visits were rare. In Paul's room, his model airplane hung in a banking climb above the darkened computer. Paul was piloting his own plane now from one development project to the next. The last Sarah had heard, he was somewhere in Argentina. In Jonathan's room, his first sculpture, a lovely nude, reclined on the dresser as comfortably as the day he had placed her there. He had been so proud of that first effort, and rightly so. Jonathan lived in the city now with his wife and two young children, adjacent to his new studio. They hadn't been out to see her in a while. Sarah had hinted that perhaps she might come in to the city for a visit this weekend, but Jonathan had demurred, saying that he was trying to finish an important project before a deadline, that they would be out to see her when they could. Of course she understood.

At the end of the hall, the desk light in her office illuminated the neat stacks of papers. It was the one light in the house she left on at night. After toiling into the small hours beneath its glow, it was always there for her when she woke before dawn, the lightship guiding her back into its harbor. On her desk, the day's priorities filled three pages of yellow pad. The computer screen blinked an urgent message from Hong Kong. A text from the Zurich office wanted her to call immediately, before the close of their business day. She found herself staring blankly at the pencil lying on the desk. A moment earlier, she had meant to pick it up, but her hand was still on the back of the chair. She switched off the light. Through the window, behind the silhouetted branches of a towering fir, the sky was shifting to a somber charcoal grey. She drifted on.

The library's fireplace was empty and cold. The leather recliner loomed in the shadows. Sometimes she could still smell the burning oak mingled with the sweet scent of pipe tobacco, and the boys would be perched on the arms of their father's chair, with little Kelly nestled into his lap, his golden baritone holding them in rapt attention as he read. Last year, Sarah had called the movers to take the chair away, but when they arrived, she wouldn't let them touch it. The chair remained, the sole monument to the years. He had taken his books with him. She had tried filling the spaces on the shelves with figurines, vases and curios.

In the great room, her finger followed the edge of the grand piano. Across the floor where she had danced, she now moved in a straight line, on through the foyer and into the dining room, hearing again the laughter of friends and the clink of champagne glasses as she passed the table. In the kitchen she circled the island, the home's heart from which all had flowed and to which all had returned—had once returned. Its veined granite lay bare and clean. The surrounding chairs, which had been nicked and worn, were repainted and re-covered. She opened the French doors to the patio—the cold splashed her face and hands, spilling around her wrists and ankles, rising beneath her robe, around her bare legs.

The morning mist had settled over the back lawn, wetting the frost. Her daily routine led down the flagstone walk to the greenhouse, where reflexively, she turned to wind through the boxwood hedges that led to the gardens, following the serpentine route that allowed inspection of each well-groomed plot. The pruning was finished. The perennials were trimmed and mulched. The tulips, larkspur and peonies had been tucked under. In the vegetable and herb beds, the clods of earth lay belly-up to the sky, awaiting the blanket of snow. There was nothing left to be done.

By the time she reached the back of the gardens, the night's shadows had dissolved in the dawn's silver twilight, which seemed to rise from the earth itself, the moon a paling wafer lingering in the haze above. Along the path through the stands of maple and birch, the moss on the trunks glistened with frosty dew, the carpet of dead leaves and rotting branches offering up the crisp pungency of decay. Ahead, the water lay like polished slate beneath the diaphanous shroud of mist veiling the lake's far shore.

She paused at the gazebo, where the swing for two hung empty and still at the end of its chains. It was there that Douglas had left her sitting, too stunned to cry. From the supply in the lidded bench she took a fresh towel and draped it over the railing. Beside the towel she draped her robe. Below the robe she arranged her slippers.

This year, the ritual of her morning swim had extended past the end of summer and on through the autumn months. She couldn't say why. The water's embrace was simply something she needed, like the light on her desk. When she reached the middle of the lake, she would float awhile, then exhale and let her body slip quietly beneath the surface to sink slowly down through the ever colder, darker depths. The feeling of the mud closing about her feet had at first sent her kicking upwards for light and air—but it was only mud, she had been telling herself, the same as the stuff in her garden beneath a rainy day, where all things that have had their season inevitably return to rest. She had been staying down longer of late.

The path to the water's edge passed through the outermost feature of her landscaping, a circular haven of evergreen hedges. She stopped there—startled.

There had always been the stone bench on the one side, but she had never found quite the right ornament for the view opposite. Her first thought was that the style of the sculpture was unmistakable—and then she couldn't think anymore because her body was straightening to match the bearing of the marble figure, an ageless beauty in a summer dress, hands resting lightly on the hips, looking out into the world with strength, resolve and a peaceful joy. Gazing at it, she could feel her son's hands gently pushing on the small of her back, pulling her shoulders, lifting her chin. It was a perfect likeness of her. It was her own lost soul, and as she stood before the vision, it filled and filled her. The base was engraved:

> *For the woman who has everything—*
> *Happy birthday, Mom.*
> *– Jonathan*

She had been standing there for longer than she knew when the morning's silence was broken by the sound of a horn from the direction of the front drive, followed by the shutting of car doors and the laughter of children—Jonathan's.

She hadn't expected them. She turned and walked briskly toward the gazebo. There was hot cocoa and muffins to be made. As she tied the belt of her robe, she glanced back to the lake. As soon as it froze over, she would be out on the ice with the children, teaching them how to skate. She removed the remaining towels from beneath the bench, tucking them beneath her arm as she turned toward the house.

Above the circle of evergreen, the first snowflake of winter drifted down, turning a fine pirouette. It came to rest on a sublime marble cheek, and melted there.

*   *   *

*

The Sculpture That Won the War

From a letter to a sculptor
Sept 27, 2001

ONCE UPON A TIME, there was a sculptor who had only the face to finish of a magnificent statue, his masterpiece to date. Frustrated by his limitations and increasingly dissatisfied with his efforts to bring into existence the perfection in his mind's eye, his progress on the artwork had foundered and stalled. His workshop had fallen silent. Indeed, as the days and weeks and months drifted on, the statue was in danger of never being finished at all.

But on a crystal-clear morning, a morning seemingly as peaceful as any other in living memory, a shocking event occurred: the sculptor's country came under attack. It was a morning of sudden and unexpected terror, of cold-blooded murder that left thousands dead and the populace reeling.

Over the next days and weeks, a miasma of insecurity and anxiety settled over the land, ubiquitous and inescapable, visible on the faces of the rich and the poor, the young and the old, the strong and the weak, the eminent and the obscure. Their sense of wellbeing had vanished overnight; their paradigm had shifted, ostensibly forever. In response to the attack, some wanted to stand and fight; others wanted to kneel and plead; most wandered through their hours fearful and confused, unsure of what to do. While the government drafted plans for war, the citizenry went about their daily routines as well as they were able, anxious for what the fractured future might bring for themselves and for their loved ones, wanting to do something, anything, to combat the pervasive sense of helplessness, yet uncertain of what, if anything, could be done.

The sculptor knew that his country was in greater need than ever of emotional fuel, and he knew what could help provide it. His country was fighting for her life—she needed vision and inspiration to survive, to defend herself, to remember what she had once been, to conquer, to rebuild, to thrive once again. With renewed vigor and determination, he threw his efforts into doing what he could do, contributing with what he did best. Days and nights, coffee and curses, dejection and perseverance, but finally—satisfaction, satisfaction that he had done what he could do, as well as he could do it.

Within a few weeks of the enemy's strike, the sculptor sent his finished clay to the foundry; within a dozen weeks thereafter, the foundry delivered the finished bronze to the gallery; the gallery, in turn, delivered the artwork to the client who had commissioned it.

The delivery brought in the balance of payment to the gallery which, due to the widespread economic uncertainties subsequent to the attack, was on the brink of closing for lack of sales. The buyer, upon receiving the sculpture, was so delighted with the finished work that he was motivated to place yet another significant commission with the gallery, and the deposit toward the new commission kept the gallery open for a few precious months more. Over that period, the economy stabilized sufficiently that regular purchases began to trickle in again, just enough that the gallery would never again be quite so close to failing.

In the spring after the sculpture was completed and delivered, an eight-year old girl was passing by the gallery with two of her friends. Upon catching a glimpse of the art on display in the window she drew her friends inside, and as they browsed the cornucopia of treasures within, the girl stopped before a lovely figure, a bronze sculpture patined in white. It was a smaller casting of the sculptor's larger masterpiece. She fell in love with it, and she was all the more enchanted and delighted when she discovered, upon reading the tag at the artwork's base, that she shared the sculpture's name. She could hardly afford the sculpture itself, of course, but she spotted a photographed image of the piece framed and hanging on the wall nearby.

It too was available for purchase. She checked the price—she couldn't afford the photograph either. But she did have five dollars. She approached the gallery manager to offer what she had, wondering, hoping. The manager dug through her filing cabinet and found, from a recent mailing campaign, a postcard that featured an image of the sculpture. She gave it to the girl, smilingly, without charge. The girl went home and slipped the postcard into the edge of the mirror on her bedroom wall.

A young pilot cruised silently through the cold night sky, the diamond dust of stars twinkling above. The blanket of clouds below stretched ahead toward a rumpling rise in the distance, marking the boundary of mountainous terrain beneath. His sortie consisted only of himself and his wingman, in two stealth fighters. According to the screen in front of him, they had just crossed the border into enemy territory. It wouldn't be long now.

The mountains ahead bristled with anti-aircraft batteries.

War had been declared on those who had supported the terrorists and their atrocious acts. The ground war was proving more difficult than anticipated, with the enemy forces scurrying back into the crevices and caves of the mountains at the slightest provocation. The enemy's military leader, the very swine who had devised and overseen the terrorist attack, was proving elusive, but a disillusioned member of his inner circle had been susceptible to bribing, and the leader's location had been leaked. The caves in which he was thought to be hiding and their surroundings had been bombed incessantly over the past days, and on this evening, an intelligence satellite had picked up a small convoy attempting to leave the area under the cover of darkness. A forward spotter on the ground confirmed that it was indeed the enemy leader, who could disappear into another system of caves within minutes or hours.

The jets had been scrambled immediately, and now the pair were within a short thirty miles of their target. They rolled onto their sides and slipped like diving nighthawks through the clouds and to the height of the peaks before turning into a craggy-walled valley. By design, the cutting-edge craft were nearly undetectable by radar, but a watchful enemy soldier, at first spooked by the two shadows streaking silently above, frantically radioed ahead a warning. Anti-aircraft fire began tracing upwards, trying to catch the fleeting apparitions. The pilots dropped lower so as not to offer a silhouette against the night sky. Without warning, a missile from below caught the wingman's craft, and it erupted into a comet of flame, dropping away without so much as a sound from the pilot's radio.

The young pilot who remained fought to stay focused. All of his reflexes wanted to pull the stick back and shoot straight up to the sky, to rise above the fiery tracings that would surely find him too at any moment, to live to fight another day.

Deep in the canyon, radio reception was intermittent and broken. He might have heard his commander's order to pull up and out, but he might not have heard it either. If he climbed, he might be able get a fair shot at the convoy from altitude—if he survived the incoming fire to which the altitude would expose him—but it was the enemy leader himself, the black heart and soul of the enemy forces, who was traveling in that convoy. When would there be another chance if the pilot missed or if he were shot down before being able to make another attempt? How long might the war drag on if the leader escaped? The images that had been seared into his memory on that accursed morning came again—the hijacked airliners crashing into the skyscrapers, the innocents plunging from the heights to their deaths, the buildings collapsing, the vacant despair on the faces of the survivors.

He thought of the postcard in the breast pocket of his flight suit, of the delicately looped handwriting in violet pen on the postcard's reverse, of the girl who had sent the accompanying letter. He switched off his radio. Steeling himself, he kicked the plane over on its side, banking hard around a canyon corner, flying lower yet, the bullets from small arms pinging into his craft's underbelly.

The infrared radar confirmed the vehicles of the convoy on the road ahead, speeding toward a pass so narrow that even if he were on his side he wouldn't be able to follow them in. He dropped lower, the dust from the road boiling in his wake. Either of the laser-guided bombs on board would get the job done, but he wouldn't be able to gain enough elevation in time to guide one in on the first pass, and he wouldn't be able to complete a second pass before the convoy scattered.

He hadn't even met the girl. She was a student in a class of fourth graders that had adopted his unit. They had sent a package of home-made baked goods and letters. Her envelope had found its way onto his bunk just the evening before. The letter opened with the generically respectful "Dear Sir—" He recalled the words written on the back of the enclosed postcard and the tiny violet heart after the girl's name. On the front of the postcard was the image of a sculpture, the embodiment of innocence and delight. It was the only mail he had received in weeks. It was enough.

"Okay, baby, this one's for you. . . ."

He armed both of the bombs and aimed the nose of his black angel at the rear vehicle in the convoy ahead. In his final seconds, he thought of the target, of the enemy leader, and realizing something, he chuckled. With the fire of hell in his eyes, he said, "Live by the plane, die by the plane, mother f—"

On a cloudless morning in the thin mountain air, an American soldier walked through the scattered wreckage at the site of the strike. Pieces of wood, metal and clothing were scattered about the perimeter of the blackened gouge in the road, three hundred yards long. It would go down in history as the place where the head of the hydra was killed and the tide of war had been turned. The platoon was combing through the wreckage for any of what might remain of the leader's papers and effects. Of the pilot's body, they hadn't been able to find anything, though small pieces of the plane were identifiable here and there. But the oddest scraps can survive such conflagrations: after the attack that had brought down the buildings and started the war, one of the terrorists' passports had been found in the rubble below.

The soldier lifted a piece of twisted metal and noticed in the ashes beneath it a postcard, its edges curled and seared brown but otherwise unburned. On the front was the photo of a sculpture, an elegant figure in white, beckoning to be followed into a world of wonder and happiness. The soldier smiled. He turned the photo over and read: "Dear Sir, this is how I used to feel before the war. I hope I can feel this way again someday. Thank you for fighting for me.—Joy"

The soldier tucked the photo into his breast pocket and slung his rifle over his shoulder. Kicking aside a half-burned turban, he walked down the road and took in a chestful of clean air. For the first time in months, he allowed himself to think of home.

* * *
*

For My Softest One

For my softest one, in a hammock of satin,
A bed of rose petals on pillows of mink.
So lightly you lie, a suspended sonata,
In lines of fine ivory and islets of pink.

Hands hollow with hunger, my fingers would follow
Each lift to its fall, each peak to its draw.
To bruise or to break I would not, yet I think
That I must, as I live, partake as I give—

Eyes careless and blue beneath cumulus climbing,
Hair tumbled and free, framing all my dream fair.
I trace your terrain, hands floating so closely,
My heat and your cool wring a tear from the air.

I dare to drift over, hold still in the hover
Till naught but sheer will stands between us until—
Dire wanting, still saving, a chasm of craving,
Distilling desire into Need to fulfill—

Still close and down closer the rain to the desert,
First drops of anointment die shushed in a steam.
Time reined and arrested, eternal and blessed,
Made holy by all that we are and do deem.

Till eyes into eyes of reflection are falling,
The moment unknown of the melting and meld.
Consumed and consuming, the magnetic dooming,
As metals once separate in oneness are weld.

Confluence of burning souls molten and churning,
Long-suffering uprooted, sucked out with the flow.
Canyons swept clean of love lost and hope fading,
Washed down to rest deep beneath new fields below.

Felled fences left lying, the festive gone feasting,
The borders abandoned, the ships left to sink,
Till I rise again, for my softest one,
In a bed of rose petals on pillows of mink.

Suite Boxes

(by the grace of J.S. Bach)

Came gift after gift, suite boxes of sixes,
Soft muffle of canon rolled in from the sea,
A fugue led us laughing through harmony hedges,
A maze to a garden delight.

The tumbles of flora, so masterfully petalled,
A founting of blue rising high till it fell.
We left the day's dress behind waterfall curtain,
Stepped through to wash memory away.

We waded cascades till the river ran deeply,
Surrendered all will to the strength of still flow,
We lay on the shore, souls quiet and shining.
The sun dried us softly to sleep.

Away once again to the place we remember,
To rest from the burden of so far to go.
A secret bridge shared to the call of sweet cello,
Hands held, we close our eyes.

The Hunter

THE CLASSROOM WINDOWS were open to the life-laden air of New England's early summer. Patches of sunlight waltzed with shadows of leaves across open textbooks and pages of notes. The young woman speaking at the head of the class paused, looking up from her lectern and over the faces on which the sun would soon fully shine.

"In summary, class, courage is a requirement for achieving and maintaining values great and small—the greater the value and the less certain its achievement, the greater the requisite courage. Courage is a concomitant of principle, a form of integrity, a necessity for achieving the proper end of all ends—man's life. . . . Next week, you will be tested on the material we covered today, but remember that you are, and will be, tested every day of your life by reality itself. Your reward for passing my test will be a good grade; your reward from reality will be the greatest happiness possible to you. Class dismissed."

A murmur of voices rose, punctuated with squeaks of desks and scrapes of moving chairs, subsiding again as the students filtered out. Two remained. A dandelion-haired girl, whose unfolding beauty had raced a day ahead of spring's pace, gathered her belongings and, after a moment's hesitation, followed her peers. An awkward boy, preoccupied ostensibly with making a few extra notes and arranging his materials, watched her leave. He unraveled his lanky frame and ambled slowly towards the door.

"David?"

"Yes, ma'am?"

"Is there anything you'd like to talk about?"

Her most intelligent and studious pupil had spent another day in class staring absently out the window and tracing distractedly in the margin of his book. His glasses, which usually magnified a bright liveliness, today revealed only clouds of frustration and melancholy.

"Ms. Ralovna, have you ever wanted something so much that you were afraid to go after it?" he asked.

She looked to an empty chair in the back corner of the room where, in another classroom, in another time, another boy had sat.

"David, do you remember the discussion we had last week about the difference between living and not dying?" She watched with delight as a pinpoint ray of understanding pierced his clouds.

"If you'll excuse me, ma'am—" His words had barely escaped a flurry of thought as he departed in an altogether altered state of distraction.

The professor collected her books and her briefcase. Before closing the door, she stopped and gazed again at the empty chair. A pair of girls who were passing in the hall at that moment waited until they were out of earshot.

"Did you see the look on her face?"

"It's my opinion that Dr. Tatiana Ralovna has a lover."

"And she's meeting him tonight."

"I wonder what he's like."

"He's probably an accountant."

"And what will they do?"

"Talk in impassioned whispers about the philosophy of mathematics."

They giggled and changed the subject to shoes.

That evening, Tatiana was curled in an armchair, her legs tucked under her and a blanket over her lap, grading her students' papers. A bookmarked novel awaited atop a stack of its cousins on the side table. With her loosened hair falling over her thin shoulders, she looked young enough to attend one of her own classes.

A key turned in the door, and she glanced up expectantly. The man entering was more than twice her age. His erect bearing, weathered skin, and quick, hawkish eyes belied the dark suit and tie; the uniform and insignia of a field commander might have been more fitting; a commander coming off the field from the battle of his life might have looked as exhausted.

"Tasha, love, I'm sorry I'm late." He kissed her forehead and embraced her.

"It's okay, Papa," she said, hiding her concern as she helped him with his coat. "Come, sit at the table. Dinner will be ready in just a moment. Sit now, and I'll bring you a drink."

"You waste too much on an old man, Tasha. When was the last time you brought a young man home to dinner? It's been months. And then you never invite them back. How am I ever to become a grandpapa?"

"You know I get bored with them," she said, setting a bourbon and water in front of him and hurrying into the kitchen. "Some have been very nice, but . . ." She looked to the back window, to the dark woods beyond, but found only her reflection in the glass.

"But you can't find a man to match the heroes in the books you read. You're too romantic, Tasha, and too picky. Your books can't keep you warm at night."

She blushed, though she hadn't been thinking of a fictional hero at all. Setting two plates of steaming stroganoff on the table, she watched her Papa eat without tasting. He often came home weary, worrying over a problem that had followed him from work, but his manner was always that of a man playing chess or solving a puzzle, knowing that it was only a matter of time before he would find the solution. Tonight, there was something in his countenance she had never seen before.

"Papa, what's wrong?"

He frowned. "You know I can't talk about it, love."

"You could tell me without really telling—without the details."

"I worry enough about you as it is, Tasha. If the wrong people ever got their hands on you, I would be their toy. And if they thought you knew anything . . ." He shook his head.

"Please, Papa, I'm a grown woman, and you need to talk."

"You deserve a younger man, love."

He kept putting the food into his mouth, the fork moving more and more slowly until finally it didn't rise again from his plate though he was hardly half finished with the portion. He was studying a dark line of wood grain in the table.

"There is evil in the world, Tasha," he announced, quietly and simply.

Tatiana lowered her utensils and picked up her wine glass.

He continued, as one forced to watch from a distance. "The president will be in Rome on Sunday. . . ."

"For the meeting with the Italian prime minister," she said. "It's been in the news." What she knew of Papa's work, from overheard snippets of phone calls over the years and elliptical discussions with associates, was only that it involved weighty issues of great import, secrets and dangerous people, matters that involved the country's security.

"You suspect that the president might be in danger?" she ventured.

"I can't suspect what I know."

That he was opening up to her, breaking his rules, made her all the more concerned. He was a cautious, highly disciplined man. But he seemed beyond his wits' end.

"Someone is going to try to kill the president?" she asked.

"He won't just try."

His calm certainty startled her. She waited, but nothing more was forthcoming.

"And that someone is evil. . . ?" she ventured.

"Those who sent him certainly are."

"But surely, Papa, if this is something you can't stop, you've told the president or his people, and he'll cancel or postpone the trip, or they'll take whatever measures are necessary to assure his safety."

"The president's people think it's ludicrous that someone could get close enough to kill him without a gun."

"Without a gun?"

"You remember last year when the ambassador to Britain was assassinated. He was in a parade and he went over to shake hands with a group of people—I've watched the video hundreds of times—the group swallows him up for a moment, and the next, he's lying on the pavement with his throat cut."

Tatiana looked down at the knife resting on the edge of her plate.

"You couldn't see who did it, Tasha, and the witnesses' descriptions were worthless. Since that day we've sent six men after the man who we think did it, and on my desk are spread the photos of six corpses, every one's throat slit as cleanly as a rabbit's."

Tatiana looked from the knife to the red wine in her hand, to the resignation in her Papa's eyes.

"The most recent photo was put on my desk this morning. It was Gary, the man I brought home to dinner last week, the one I thought you might take a liking to. He was the best man I had left, Tasha. Last night he sent a message from a town near Rome saying that he was on the trail of the Hunter."

The glass slipped from her hand and shattered against the edge of the table, splashing wine across the floor as she stood abruptly.

"I am so sorry, Tasha," he said, rising to help her. "You're unaccustomed to all this death and gore. Dinner certainly wasn't the place to discuss it."

"What did you say his name is again?" she asked.

"Gary."

"No, the killer."

"We don't know his name. We have no idea what he looks like. We know that those who sent him refer to him only as the Hunter."

Tatiana was standing motionless in the pool of wine.

"Come, Tasha, let's get this cleaned up. Please don't worry. There has to be a way to stop him. I just haven't found it yet."

She went through the motions of cleaning the floor and clearing the table. Papa went up to his room, leaving her alone in the kitchen. She picked up a carving knife and turned it over in her hands, watching the light glint from its sharp edge. Replacing it on the counter, she went quietly upstairs to her room. It took ten minutes to call the airport and pack an overnight bag. As she slipped out she could see, under Papa's door, his shadow moving slowly back and forth as the unknown and unheralded commander struggled for a strategy. On the dining room table she left a note:

"Dearest Papa—I'm going away for the weekend to see an old friend. Please don't worry. Love you—Tasha."

* * *

The lights on the land below gave way to the ocean's moonlit shimmering. In the plane's darkened cabin the only movement was a shadowed figure walking farther up the aisle. Tatiana leaned back in her seat, closed her eyes and let the years slip away, remembering. . . .

The boy had been walking far ahead of her along a footpath that wound through a forested aisle of black trees and dense underbrush. The cries of birds settling for the evening in the branches above joined the rising cacophony of insects on the forest floor. The occasional rustling of dead leaves and the snapping of twigs marked the stirrings of larger things. She resolved not to fall too far behind.

He was the one who sat behind her in the back corner of class, taller than the other boys and lean, with muscles like steel cords running through his arms. His clothes were handmade, of a smooth, tough leather. His alert, untroubled eyes registered the other students in the same sweep as they did the twittering birds beyond the classroom window.

One day he had come into class late and, sitting down at his desk, laid a dead rabbit with his books on the floor. The sniggering and whispers of the other students fell silent when the Professor, caressing the handle of his ever-present crop, asked—

"Why are you tardy?"

The boy held up the rabbit, its throat cut in a clean, straight line.

"I was hunting," he answered guiltlessly, in a tone that questioned the question.

After a long, silent appraisal, the Professor laid the crop aside and, from that moment on, took a keen interest in the boy's academic progress. The other students now had their nickname for the one who it was rumored always wore a knife strapped to his leg. One day, Tatiana summoned the courage to ask him about the knife. She received only his cool silence in response.

Unable to learn more about him at school, she was attempting, that evening, to follow him home through the forest, keeping far enough behind that she would see him again only just before he disappeared around the next turn.

A ball of brown fur tumbled into the path in front of her, and she found herself looking down into the inquisitive face of a small bear cub, only a few weeks old. Enchanted, she bent low and held out her hand. The cub came sniffing towards her. A twig snapped under her toe—the startled cub yelped, and a crash of breaking branches brought the mother bear rearing high over her with a furious roar that ended in a scream—the scream of a boy. The bear twisted to meet the blade-tipped arc of the Hunter's leap, and the flash of metal disappeared as it flew across the massive neck. The boy landed in a crouch between the girl and the bear, and the fire in the beast's eyes went cold as it crumpled into a harmless mass of fur and flesh.

Tatiana was sitting in the dirt where she had fallen. The boy turned from the bear to look down at her, his examination starting at her bare, thorn-scraped legs and moving up her body until it found the pounding pulse in her throat. When his eyes met hers, the simple expectation she saw in them frightened her as badly as had the bear, and she found her feet and ran until she was safely locked behind her bedroom door.

The next morning, wearing a fresh white blouse and a newly creased blue skirt, she was waiting by the school gate. The boy emerged from the forest path onto the school road, and when all but a few straggling students had gone inside and she was sure that he had seen her, she slipped along the base of the wall and around the corner.

The school was a converted monastery, an ancient, prodigious complex of crumbling stone, iron gratings and onion-domed turrets. Along the bottom of one of the back walls, where the stone was collapsing under its own weight, was a hole hidden behind the brush and a pile of rocks. Most of the students knew of the hole's existence. Few had dared enter it. Stories were told of tombs beneath the school, of skulls and bones, of children who had ventured in but never returned, of a domed room with an altar that had once been used for human sacrifice in secret rites. Tatiana climbed over the rocks, cutting her knee on an edge of mortar, and slipped down into the darkness.

She found herself in a small room with a dirt floor, low ceiling and cobwebbed corners. Other than a pair of rusted chains hanging from one of the walls, some scattered rat droppings, and a few small animal bones, the space was bare. From an arched opening ahead came a cool, wet breeze. A rock turned outside. She glanced quickly around—this was hardly an altar room.

The arched opening led into a narrow passageway punctured with smaller arched openings along each side. What little light that followed her down the passageway vanished as she went deeper. The air chilled, and the stone walls, which had been dry at the opening, became webbed with rivulets of moisture and patches of sticky fuzziness. Her face hit a wall in front of her. Beneath the dim arch behind her, a silhouette moved.

The wet air seemed to be coming from her right—she shivered and, as much feel as by sight, found an opening to the left. A short flight of steps led up from the cold to a passage that was even narrower, the openings along its sides shorter. She caught the next wall ahead with her hand, but this time she could go no further—it was a dead end. From the blackness behind came only a distant, echoing drip. She felt her way back to one of the side openings and pushed open a wooden door, its hinges squealing horribly as she ducked inside.

A coin-sized hole near the top of the opposite wall allowed a feeble, dusky light to spread through what appeared to have been a monk's cell. The remains of a rough wooden desk and chair lay in a corner. A crudely carved crucifix was propped in a niche above. She toed at a heap of rotted leather—sheets of crumbling parchment tumbled across the floor. Inset in the wall across from the desk and chair was a shelf of stone, waist high and just long and deep enough for a short man to lie on.

A hand over her mouth stopped her scream. The boy turned her slowly around and relaxed his hold as she fell silent. In the gray light his face was stoic and hard, except for his parted lips. She closed her eyes, waiting, shivering as his fingers slid from her mouth to her throat, then around her neck and into her hair, pulling her head back and lifting her mouth to his. His lips brushed her cheek. His teeth tested her lower lip. Her blouse was slipped open and her shoulders were bared, the sleeves pulled down around her elbows, pinning back her arms. She found herself against the edge of the shelf—he lifted her by her waist to sit on it. Then she was lying back as his hands discovered whatever they would, whatever they wanted.

A blinding light shattered their vision—Tatiana clutched her blouse to her chest.

"There you are, my son." It was the Professor's voice behind the light. There were two older students flanking him. "And what have you found more interesting than attending class this morning? Ah, I see. I must say that I am disappointed. The other students in your class are having to wait on their lessons due to your pursuit of your selfish, animal desires. But I see that you are only partly to blame. Today, the Hunter has been the prey, lured into the oldest of traps. Go back to class now, my son. We shall discuss this later."

"Yes, Professor . . ."

The boy hesitated, waiting for her, but the professor motioned him and the other students along. When Tatiana tried to follow, the professor stopped her with the light to her eyes.

"Not just yet, Miss Tatiana. I will deal with you now." He unbuttoned his shirt sleeves and rolled them up to his elbows as he waited for the footsteps to fade. "Now turn around and place your hands on your filthy bed."

She turned slowly, trying to watch him over her shoulder, lowering one hand but clutching her blouse to her chest with the other.

Her back arched at the crop's fire. She fought to stifle a cry. She didn't want the boy to hear.

"Drop the other hand, you little whore, or you'll suffer worse than the crop."

She lowered her blouse to the stone and closed her eyes.

When they returned to the classroom, the professor unrolled his sleeves and put his coat back on.

"And now that we're all present," he announced, with an air of satisfaction—"There will be a change in the lesson plan today. Our lecture will concern the character and discipline required of a citizen to do his duty, to sacrifice everything—his carnal desires, his dearest possessions, his family, even his own life if necessary—for the common good, for the greatest good, for the good of the People. . . ."

Tatiana, feeling her blouse stick to her back, bit her lip and pressed back hard against the slats of her chair. Then she leaned forward and held her head high, knowing that the boy who sat in the corner behind her would see the stripes of her flag.

It was that night, upon seeing the blood and the bruises, that the man she had come to call Papa decided that he had had enough, that it was time to return to his own country—and to take her with him, if her mother would allow. She remembered hearing him say, "The girl will never survive here, and if she survives, she won't live." How right he had been, she realized years later. She had known nothing of his work then, only that he was from a distant, wonderful place, and that she was never to reveal his secret to anyone.

That night he had said goodbye to his lover, and the lover to her daughter. At the border, she had been sure that the guards could hear the pounding of her heart through the crates and potato sacks behind which she was hidden, but Papa was there with her, holding her hand, and she focused on slowing her breathing as he had taught her to do when frightened. Then they were through the border and on to the darkened landing strip. Her fear fell away as they went flying high above the moonlit ocean to her new home, the land of the free.

That had been half her lifetime ago. She opened her eyes and looked down through the plane's window, but there was only the darkness below and the distant skitter of lightning across the horizon. She reached for Papa's hand, but he wasn't there. She wondered if the boy remembered.

Rome's mid-afternoon was heavy with humidity. Dropping her bag on the hotel bed, she picked up the phone on the side table.

"Operator, the American embassy, please."

She brushed a lock of hair out of the perspiration and dust on her forehead.

"Hello? Yes, this is Dr. Tatiana Ralovna. I'm a U.S. citizen, and

I'm here hunting for an old friend. I would like to leave my location with you in case he tries to get in touch. . . . Yes, it's—" she repeated her name slowly, followed by her hotel and room number, enunciating clearly for whoever would be monitoring calls coming in to the embassy. From what she had gleaned from Papa's conversations, she was confident that her appearance in Rome would soon be known to those to whom it would be of most interest. After the call, she changed into a white blouse and a blue knee-length skirt, fixed her make-up and hair, and went downstairs. At an outdoor cafe beside the hotel, she found an empty table by the wall and selected a chair facing the piazza.

A stooped, elderly couple strolled slowly by, hand in hand. A waddling toddler clung to an extended finger, multiplying his father's steps by four. Through the weaving scooters and honking cars, pairs of lovers could be seen lounging around the piazza's marble fountain. When the waiter came, she ordered a glass of wine. Donning her sunglasses, she leaned her head back against the wall and closed her eyes for a few moments' rest.

On an otherwise deserted street corner halfway across town, a man indistinguishable from the locals in attire and manner approached a payphone, checking his watch with apparent nonchalance. He dialed a number, let it ring eleven times, then hung up the phone, checked his wristwatch, and waited. His body language communicated to anyone who might be watching that he was bored, uninterested, perhaps a little irritated, but from behind his dark glasses, he scanned the street, taking in everything that moved and most of what didn't. Exactly twenty-two seconds later, the phone rang. He answered without a greeting, in a dialect known only to those from his native village and the few villages surrounding.

"This is highly unusual," he said.

"I had to speak to you directly. They have sent another."

"The plan and schedule is set. I will be in place in three hours. No one can—"

"Do you remember the girl beneath the school?"

There was a long silence.

"Are you there?"

"Yes."

"Well?"

"I remember."

"She arrived in Rome this afternoon. She's the only one who could identify you tomorrow. We must believe now that they have become aware of your presence here. They're using her for bait, trying to draw you out. They wanted us to hear that she is 'hunting' for an old friend. She is in the open now, sitting in front of the café on the Piazza dei Campanili. It is a trap, yet she must not be available to identify you tomorrow."

The man at the payphone did not respond. Many years had passed, yet he knew he would recognize her, no matter how differently her hair might look or what she might be wearing or how she had grown and matured. He wondered if she would recognize him. He was no longer the boy he had been. He had done many things over the years at the direction of the voice on the other end of the line, but he had done what he had been told was right, what he had believed was right. . . . Yet he wondered if the girl he had known would recognize him. He wondered if the boy he had been would recognize the man—

"Are you there?" the voice interrupted.

"Yes . . ."

"You hesitate."

"No . . ."

"Do you know what you must do?"

Silence.

"You have demonstrated time and again your willingness to risk your safety and well-being for the People, but all of those other times will be nothing in comparison to this. The path must be cleared for your action tomorrow. Nothing must be allowed to threaten the outcome."

Silence.

"Do you know what you must do?"

"What must I do?"

"You know the answer to that question—you will do what is necessary. The woman will use innocent eyes, enticing words, and her sex, the spider watching for your moment's hesitation to close the web. But you have learned to conquer all desire. You will not hesitate. You will not fail your duty. You will rise to sacrifice that which was once dear to you. Tomorrow will be a great victory for the People, but today will be the greatest victory for you by far, my son."

Silence.

"Do you know what you must do?"

"You will tell me."

"Kill the bitch."

Silence.

"Do you hear me, my son?"

"Yes, Professor."

The sky over the piazza's fountain had grown dark. With a rumble of thunder, the first drops of rain sent the pedestrians scattering. On the opposite side of the piazza, beneath an awning, Tatiana saw a low-brimmed hat atop a long gray raincoat. She shivered as a cool breeze brushed her arms. She couldn't see the face, but she was sure he was studying her. Finishing with a swallow what remained of her wine, she hailed a taxi.

"Drive south, please."

A few blocks later she looked behind and saw a black car come around the corner from the square.

Her driver hadn't spoken a word. He too was wearing dark glasses, though the gathering storm had cast an early twilight. She noticed that he was spending more time watching the rearview mirror than the road ahead. And he had understood her English perfectly well.

Before she could gather the nerve to jump from the vehicle, she was thrown violently against the taxi's door as the driver cornered sharply into a side street and gunned the engine. She screamed.

"Hey! Take it easy, lady," the driver yelled, his accent thick and rolling. "Do not scare me like that!"

"Who are you and where are you taking me?"

"I am the best damned driver in this city—and you are a beautiful American woman—and I will be damned if I will let anyone get you. Hang on, lady!" He floored the accelerator and the taxi shot ahead as pedestrians leaped aside and cyclists cursed.

"But I *want* to be followed."

"Oh?" The cab screeched to a stop. "Well you should have said so." He threw the car in reverse and backed up the street nearly as fast as he had gone down it. She braced herself as he braked to another screeching stop.

"There you go, lady. See? Now they are much closer, right where you want them. I am the best damned driver in the city and they will not be able to lose me again. Do you want to keep going south?"

"Yes, please," she sighed.

The black car dropped back until she could no longer see it through the rain-streaked glass.

"He is still there, don't you worry," the driver said. He turned up the radio and bobbed his head to a disco tune, sporadically blurting out a mangled English lyric.

They passed through the ruins of one of the city's ancient gates, beyond which the sparse buildings gave way to broken, hilly meadows, dark purple mounds in the murky twilight. The driver turned off the radio when the signal faded.

"The catacombs are out here, aren't they?" she asked.

"They are all over this area, lady, and they find new ones all the time. It is like a huge web of—how do you call them?—caves. Scary enough to visit in the daytime, but I would not be caught dead in them on a night like this. Hey, that was a joke, lady—would not be caught dead in the catacombs?"

"Let me out here, please."

"Here? But there is nothing out here."

"Here."

He pulled the car to the side of the road. She heard a click of metal and saw the barrel of a pistol over the seat. She was wrestling frantically with the door handle when she saw that he was handing the gun to her handle first.

"You are awfully nervous, lady. I thought you might want this for protection. I don't know who your friend is back there, but a beautiful woman like you, out here all alone? It works very well—I use it all the time to help people pay their fares. I will give it to you for much less than it is worth—two hundred American dollars."

"Thank you, but I'll be fine." She searched her skirt pocket for the fare while watching the road behind them.

"One hundred and fifty, then."

She shook her head.

"Then just take it for free. No charge. You can return it to me later. I will give you my phone number." He lifted an eyebrow.

"Thank you, but no."

"Then I will stay here to guard you."

"I don't think that that would be in your best interest, sir, but thank you anyway." She gave him a generous tip.

"Okay, lady," he shrugged, raising his hands in defeat. "It's your life."

Tatiana was left standing in the mud on the side of the road, the cold rain soaking through her clothes. As the taxi sped back towards the city, the black car inched over the horizon. She waded through a ditch of knee-high water and made her way to a place between two small hills where passing traffic wouldn't be able to see her, but where someone looking for her would. She faced the road and waited.

"Yes," she echoed quietly, "it's my life."

With a crack of thunder, the rain came down with renewed urgency. The chrome bumper led the rest of the black car into view. It stopped, and for a long while there was no other movement. Then the driver's door opened, and the hat and gray coat emerged. The man walked to edge of the ditch. A flash of lightning illuminated his face. It wasn't her Hunter.

By the time the thunder reached her, she was running at full speed. There was nowhere to hide in the grassy mounds—no fences, no brush, no boulders. She dodged from one empty hollow to the next until finding the first viable escape, an excavated hole in the earth from which protruded a handmade ladder. It creaked and sagged as she descended, the rotting wood barely supporting her weight. At the bottom was a passageway down which she ran as far as the light would take her.

The vaulted catacomb was lined with tiered rows of gaping, body-sized cavities, some of which were still occupied with bones. From behind her came a snap of breaking wood, a dull thud, and a muttered curse. She pushed ahead, feeling her way through the darkness as the tunnel curved in a long, slow arc back toward the road. A faint glow ahead started her running again, but she tripped awkwardly, twisting her ankle as she sprawled to the floor. After a quick, futile search for her lost shoe, she removed the other, flung it aside and ran on, limping for the light.

A flight of crumbling stone steps led up and into the night. The rain had stopped, though the clouds still roiled threateningly. Beyond the catacomb entrance another flight of steps climbed an exposed slope beyond, a hill littered with fallen pillars and scattered slabs of broken marble. Her lungs burned as she ascended. Her ankle was on fire. In the distance below, a cargo truck lumbered by and disappeared into the night—the road was near, yet much too far away. Her breath ragged, she paused to glance behind her.

The gray coat appeared at the mouth of the catacomb.

She struggled to climb the remaining steps to the summit, where a large, half-buried block of marble lay, its edges worn by millennia of weather. When she reached it, there was nowhere else to go. She turned. The gray coat was climbing towards her, unhurried now, the hat brim tilted in line with the steps. She leaned back against the marble, waiting, watching him come, slowing her breathing as Papa had taught her to do.

The hat tilted back suddenly as a blade of reflected light flashed below it, and the coat crumpled heavily to the ground.

Her knees buckled as she slid down the stone. A black form stepped over the body and ascended deliberately, stopping only a few steps below her. A distant flicker in the storm lit the face of her Hunter. Though older, he was the same, even more so.

"Who was it?" he asked, in their native tongue.

"I don't know."

"He was using you to find me."

"I don't know."

He drew closer and stood over her, her body huddled and shivering beneath her wet clothes.

"You don't even have a weapon," he said.

She pushed herself up to standing, bracing her hands on the edge of the marble.

"Do I need one?"

"You shouldn't have come, Tatiana. You've given me no choice."

"You always have a choice."

"No," he said, looking away, turning the knife in his hand, its blade dark and wet. "It is duty."

A beam of light shot up from the road and caught them. The policeman saw a woman throw her arms around a man and lay her head against his chest. The light snapped off and the policeman drove on. Tatiana looked up into eyes where a storm raged far worse than the one around them.

"You would be killing yourself," she said.

"Then I will find the courage to die."

The moon found a rift in the clouds, turning the marble pale blue. She felt a cold, sharp line on her throat.

"It takes more courage to live," she whispered.

"Yet you sacrifice your life trying to save your president."

"The president? Oh, no, not the president. I came for you. I want to take you home."

He looked down into a face that had lost all fear and that was even—happy. Lowering the knife, he lifted her in his arms and carried her down to the road below.

A short distance away they found the car, the keys still in the ignition. Leaving his motorcycle in a ditch, he drove them back towards the city, turning on the car's heat to warm her. On an abandoned side road, he pulled over to the shoulder, and they sat and talked long into the night. Dawn was breaking when they passed back through the ancient gate and stopped at the first payphone.

"Hello, Papa?"

"Tasha? Thank God! What in hell are you doing in Rome? I've got someone following you, and I want you on the next flight home. You could be in danger—"

"As for whoever was following me, Papa, we'll have to talk about that. As for coming home—okay, but I'm bringing company. It's a man."

"You went to Rome to find a man? This is rather sudden, Tasha. I wish I would have known, but—a man? But of course, I will welcome him like a son. Tell me about this man. Who is he?"

"I can tell you nothing, Papa. He can tell you everything."

"You are starting to sound like me, Tasha, talking in riddles. What is his name?"

"I still don't know his name. It's the Hunter."

"This is not a good joke, Tasha. You know I would kill to get my hands on that bastard."

"It's not a joke, Papa, and you won't have to kill. But there will be a few conditions. . . ."

It was the end of class again. The students had handed in their tests, and most had already left the room. Her gangly scholar had sat in a different place this time, next to the girl with dandelion hair who now accompanied him towards the door. The two were chatting softly, and both wore an unmistakable glow.

"David?"

"Yes, ma'am?"

The girl went on, glancing back at him before going out.

"David, I haven't looked at your test yet, but from what I can tell, you've done rather well with the practical application."

A flush rose on the boy's cheeks. "Ma'am, we studied together for three hours last night! If you only knew the nerve it took for me to speak to her for the first time. . . ."

Tatiana saved her smile until he had left, and she looked to the back corner of the room, where sat a man, absorbed in the class textbook, which she had written.

*   *   *

*

Clever Girl

Clever girl, fräulein fair,
A mother's eyes, brimmed with care,
Swallow deep and swallow sweet
The fountain rising at your feet.

Tongue the wine and bite the beast,
Swirl the cup of earthly feast,
Dance until the dancing's through,
Then lie thee down in fields of blue.

Lie thee down and open, dear,
For breath's caress on nape and ear,
Whispers dark and purple red,
Fingers finding voids unfed.

Teething trace to hallowed vale,
Lips to begging lips inhale,
Rising storm to bursting sky,
Raindrops fall from fluttered eye.

Swallow deep and swallow sweet,
Quiet rain to cool the heat,
Earthly peace and stars above,
Worries washed away by love.

Sheltered

H E STOOD AT THE BOTTOM of the corrugated metal shaft, looking up at the sealed hatch cover above. A bare bulb threw hard shadows down on the twelve rungs of steel rebar leading to the surface. Droplets of condensed humidity clung to blooms of rust on the ladder's welds. The welds, like him, weren't perfect, but they were strong, they would hold. He had made them himself.

He adjusted the gas mask over his face, tightening the bands and checking for leaks as he blinked and closed his eyes against the perspiration trickling from his forehead. Beneath the hazmat suit, his clothing was damp. The knee-deep water in which he stood had sloshed into his rubber boots. His breathing had shallowed, quickening as the pulse pounded in his ears. It had been a year and six days since he had sealed the hatch cover above. A year and six days, but today was the day and this was the hour—now was the time. He would be courageous. He wouldn't hesitate.

From somewhere within him a paroxysm of fear welled up and shook his core, trembling through his abdomen and pushing at the back of his knees—but he remained standing.

A year and six days underground without sunlight or breeze or contact with the world above—whatever might be left of the world above. A year and six days without touch, without unrecorded voice, without contact, without friends or family. If only they had listened, if only they had been ready. But he—he had prepared. He was Reginald B. Wakefield, and he hadn't died. A wave of vindication washed over him, lifting and sweeping away all doubt and fear. He had been *right*. He raised his eyes again to the hatch cover above.

He had been right.

When he had started building the shelter in his backyard, his neighbors hadn't laughed. Many undoubtedly would have laughed or would have shaken their heads reprovingly had they known of what he was doing. But they hadn't known. It was one of the first rules he had learned from the websites and the books—to be exceptionally careful about whom, if anyone, you let know of your disaster preparations, for neighbors can become very unneighborly when they and their own children are starving. If they know of your provisions and preparations, some will resort to taking whatever they need, using whatever means necessary to do so, and all of your preparations will have served only to have made you and your family a target.

He and his eldest son, Mark, had carried out the excavation by hand, with shovels, buckets, a block-and-tackle rig and a wheelbarrow. They hauled off the dirt at night in the back of his pick-up truck, covering the growing hole in the back lawn with a large tarp. For privacy he had added two extra feet to the top of his back fence: his next-door neighbor, Ron, whose backyard barbeques were a regular feature in the neighborhood on summer weekends, was friendly enough, but was as inquisitive as he was talkative—he had been particularly difficult to throw off of the scent. Given the difficulty of deflecting Ron's questions, speculations, and unremitting interest in lending his advice on whatever his neighbor might be working on, Reginald had found it necessary to suspend his habit of borrowing from Ron's considerable collection of tools.

Anyone who might catch a glimpse of the tarp or the workings through the house's rear windows were told that an in-ground swimming pool was being built. The neighborhood children, who had been banned from playing in the backyard during construction, were disappointed the next summer to find that the large hole had been filled in and covered with new turf, but they were thrilled soon thereafter, as were his own children, when Reginald installed an above-ground pool over the spot. The pool was something of a luxury, but he justified the expense: the attached pump-house provided perfect camouflage for the shelter's ventilation ducting, and the pool itself could provide a source of emergency water. He installed a separate drain from the pool, accessible from within the shelter below; a mesh screen in the pool's vinyl cover allowed for the collection of rainwater if and as needed.

When he had first told Mark of his intent to build the shelter, Mark had been more than eager to assist, to his father's pleasant surprise. The boy had never before shown any enthusiasm for work of any sort, but through the long months of the excavation, he proved to be an unflagging and inexhaustible partner. Reginald couldn't have been more proud of his son: it was from good stock such as this that the land would be repopulated someday—and it could have been, if only Mark had survived. If only he had listened. If only he had stayed the course.

Reginald still held out some small hope that his son had somehow found adequate shelter somewhere above. As it was, Reginald would have to find another wife. She would be young and pretty and willing, and she would trust him wholeheartedly, the way younger women do. Being a survivor herself, she would understand and appreciate his wisdom and foresight, and she would never question him—not the way Margaret had. With Margaret it had become worse than questioning really, especially towards the end.

At the outset of his preparedness efforts his wife had been accepting, even proud of him—he remembered her saying so—but it seemed almost immediately she had begun questioning the scale of what he considered adequate preparation. She had been supportive of his stocking a few shelves in the garage with a couple of weeks' worth of extra food and water for their family of five, along with first-aid supplies and such, and of having a written plan to follow in the event of an emergency, but she had balked at the cost of the large generator he wanted to buy, holding out for the purchase of a smaller, less expensive model. In the end, she had surrendered to his persistence, though the acquisition had meant shortening the family's vacation to the lake that summer.

He gradually committed nearly a quarter of their two-car garage to the growing cache of emergency stores, but even this space wasn't large enough to contain the vision to which his ambitions were rising—not less than a full year's supply of food rations, water, medical supplies, batteries, propane, iodine tablets and other survival necessities such as gas masks, a water filtration system, gardening implements, woodworking tools, weapons and ammunition. Margaret's discovery of his purchase of twenty bushels of seed grain and vegetable seed had apparently proved a tipping point for her. They had argued and fought over it all night. It was true that their house stood on less than a quarter of an acre, in a suburban neighborhood, and that between the two of them they could barely keep the flowers alive in the planters on the front porch, but Reginald had been convinced by his new friends on the internet boards that seed would be worth its weight in gold in the event of societal breakdown and more tradable than most commodities. By dawn he had worn her down again, and from that day forward she had largely held silent on the subject—tolerating his "hobby" as she called it—as long as he promised not to spend too much more money on it and would continue to make time to attend the children's school functions and extracurricular activities.

But the preparations continued to cost more money and more time.

It was beyond him to comprehend how his wife could not be as concerned as he was for the safety of their family, particularly given that they lived only fifteen miles, and downwind, from the nuclear power plant. For any reasonable person, it seemed only sensible to fear that a natural disaster, accident or terrorist attack might cause a leak or explosion at the plant, and that rolling clouds of lethal radiation could engulf the town. To Reginald, there was almost nothing more fearsome than radiation, all the more so because the threat was unseen. And a nuclear disaster was hardly the only or even the worst danger to be worried about—there was every sort of potential natural disaster that might occur and the consequences of the impending economic collapse. He tried to convince Margaret to read some of his books and to watch the videos he had purchased. She had been happy enough to go to the shooting range with him to learn how to handle a handgun, and she had become proficient at doing so, but she obviously didn't grasp the full reality and peril of the coming times—or she couldn't or she didn't want to. He was unsuccessful in convincing her to watch more than the first two parts of the *Wintering the Fall* video series, and she had finished less than a hundred pages of *Surviving Hell's Fan* before returning to her novels and cookbooks.

But the more he read on the internet, the more he was convinced that a single card pulled from beneath the country's increasingly fragile structure could bring everything crashing down, leaving a virtual hell on earth. The catalyst to collapse might be another banking and financial crisis, or a massive solar flare taking out all the electronics, or widespread food shortages due to drought and high fuel costs. There were far too many vulnerable fault lines—the fragility of the economic and monetary system, an aging transportation infrastructure, the vulnerable power grids and information systems, the unchecked influx of immigrants, a federal government that seemed bent on tyranny, cultural strife wherever one turned, and always the anarchists in the wings, waiting and willing for a chance to unleash destruction. The downfall was coming—it wasn't a matter of if, but of when, and the when was surely much sooner than the naïve and gullible public were being led to believe.

For Reginald, the imminent collapse and the imperative to prepare for it were becoming two certainties in a world of uncertainty, twin pillars of truth through which there opened a path to salvation that was sure and free from doubt. With each step he took in the light of his new purpose, he grew bolder in his convictions, thriving on his budding sense of efficaciousness in the face of a miasmic future.

But then there was Margaret. Smiling, happy, contented Margaret. His wife's buoyant optimism and unflappable practicality disappointed and disturbed him deeply, and he had continued, in subtle ways, to try to inform her, to open her eyes to the truth. He left certain websites open on his computer so that she might see and be influenced by them. On the kitchen counter, he strategically left magazines and newspapers open to articles that alluded forebodingly to cataclysmic times ahead. Surely only a Pollyanna could believe that the country wasn't on the brink of implosion, but his wife's response, or lack thereof, frustrated him deeply. Margaret was certainly intelligent. Why couldn't she take the dangers as seriously as he? Why wouldn't she? She would quote statistics on the safety of nuclear power relative to coal, to gas and even to driving across town, and on the economy she would hold forth on the difference between concern and worry, maintaining that the former was proper and often justified but that the latter was wasteful and counterproductive. It was all niggling semantics to Reginald's ear. Margaret claimed to be "appropriately concerned, adequately resourceful and ultimately unafraid." *Ultimately unafraid?* What could that even mean?

And so it had surprised him when she was supportive of his desire to build a rudimentary storm shelter. "That would be prudent," she had replied cheerfully, as she took another sip of wine and continued her study of a recipe for lamb stew.

His internet research revealed a broad offering of pre-manufactured shelters available for purchase, but his budget was limited, and besides, the thought of building the shelter himself strummed the chords of his inner longing for greater independence and self reliance. As he explored the various designs for a homemade shelter, it became increasingly clear, as he read the reviews and opinions of those far more knowledgeable than he, that while a simple, relatively inexpensive shelter might save the family from an initial nuclear blast or a tornado, such would hardly serve for protection for more than a few days, or a week or two at most. How long might the family need to be able to shelter in place if radiation contaminated everything above? What about surviving a long-term famine or an epidemic or riots or marauding gangs after societal breakdown? To be truly prepared, it would be necessary, at the very least, to move all the emergency supplies underground and to fashion a shelter that was livable for an extended period—for a year at minimum, he decided. His acquaintances and advisors on the internet approved.

With Mark at his side, he had started work on the project in the early spring. Every available evening and weekend, weather permitting, they excavated, and when the weather was too poor for digging, Reginald was researching and soliciting construction and design advice from his resources. The footprint for the shelter, cleared after four months of exhausting labor, was a third of the area of the house itself, with the hole as deep as the house was tall. By autumn, he had poured the slab and had commenced the laying of the reinforced block walls.

Unlike Margaret, Mark unquestioningly trusted his father's judgment, believing everything his father told him about the magnitude of the dangers they faced. He stopped going to band practice, to his mother's dismay, and gave up his position on the school's baseball team, to his father's approval, in order to devote as much time as possible to the shelter's construction. As one of the "men of the family," as Reginald had begun referring to the two of them, Mark traveled with his father to a preparedness convention in the next state, where in a hall packed with booths and displays, he met other boys and girls whose families were equally enthusiastic about surviving an apocalypse. Among the people they met there he discovered an alluring sense of community that he had never experienced at school, where he had never been more than a shy and awkward outsider. At the convention, everyone was an outsider and all outsiders were insiders. Afterwards, he stayed in communication with several of his new friends, at least for a while.

More than anything, he loved going with his father to the shooting range, and he learned to break down, clean and reassemble their rifle and two handguns quickly and proficiently. He even became the better marksman of the two, though he was only just on par with his mother, who accompanied them to the range only two or three times a year and teased that if the men of the family went shooting a little less often, perhaps their arms might be less tired and they might shoot as well as she.

Reginald had patched together his own shelter design from the many dozens of plans he had studied, and through the building of it, it was his intention to teach his son basic carpentry, plumbing, electric and ventilation—though it was necessary to learn a fair amount of the skills and knowledge himself, on the fly. He had never really built anything of substance before, and there were more than a few hard lessons learned along the way. Some of the mistakes had been costly. By the time he laid the third row of block, the walls were out of level, for which he tried to compensate but ended up having to break them all down and start over. Later, it was necessary to redo much of the plumbing due to having used mismatched piping materials. He had come close to electrocuting himself when he forgot to turn off the main power before trying to rewire a reversed switch, only to realize later that he had merely installed the switch upside down. Through it all, he refused to consider allowing a contractor to come onto the property—one loose set of lips in the community could compromise everything.

The construction costs continued to mount, but he couldn't afford to bolster his income by putting in extra hours at his job at the printing press, which would have left even less time to work on the shelter, and there weren't enough hours in the day for that as it was. Indeed, to stay on schedule, he had declined several requests by his manager to work overtime when the press was under deadline. It had even been necessary to take several unscheduled days off from work when pouring the shelter's slab, which turned out to be more time-consuming than he had anticipated.

He applied for a new credit account so as to not upset Margaret or her household budget, deflecting her questions regarding the expenses, allowing her to believe that he was using money he had tucked away over the years. It wasn't difficult to rationalize that worrying much about how long it might take to pay off the account or about the potential risk to the family's credit simply wasn't worth it: what good would having good credit be when the banks and the financial system crashed?

He missed many of Peter's soccer practices and games while finishing the shelter's walls and trying to maneuver the ceiling trusses into place before the second load of cement was scheduled for delivery. He missed Amanda's school play while relocating the generator to its underground compartment. Margaret had found herself alone at a parent-teacher meeting regarding Mark's slumping grades while her husband was at an estate sale in the next town, bidding on a shortwave radio set. Reginald remembered their seventeenth wedding anniversary—a week late.

But with his new focus and commitment, he had begun to feel like a man again in a world in which, over the years, he had come to feel increasingly ineffectual. There was a newborn pride in his soul, swaddled in the conviction that he was one of the exceptional few who could see a future that others could not. One day, if he persevered, he would be counted as one of the men who had seen, one of the men who had taken action. His family would be among those who would endure to rebuild the world and to stand strong in whatever the aftermath might bring. Few of the unprepared might survive, and those who did would find themselves dependent on men like himself—the men who had prepared.

The main living area of the shelter included a kitchenette and a small dining and sitting area with library shelves, a television, a computer station and the shortwave radio. The second room stored the dried and canned foods, the first-aid, cleaning and survival supplies, farming implements, bags of seed, a grain mill, tools, extra clothing, gas masks, hazmat suits, spare parts, light bulbs, toiletries and other sundry provisions. Firearms and ammunition were kept in a padlocked cabinet. A compost toilet and a wash basin were installed in a closet off of the main room. In the third and smallest room, five bunks were built against the walls, with the top bunks hinged so that they could be raised during waking hours, leaving the lower bunks available for extra seating.

Ten months after groundbreaking, their fourth child, Isabelle, was born. It was too late to expand the shelter—Reginald decided that the baby could sleep at first with Margaret and later either with Martha or on a pallet on the floor made up with spare clothing.

Recessed in the wall of the sleeping quarters, hidden behind a mirror, was a compartment for money, records and critical papers. It was Reginald's fervent wish to add some gold and silver bullion to the cache, but given the priority of other expenses it was not yet within his means to do so. He purchased a ventilation system with blast valves and special filters that promised to protect against nuclear, biological and chemical contamination—the system was the company's top-line package and not inexpensive, but as the video on the company's website reminded, all of his other expenditures and supplies would be worthless to his family if he didn't provide safe air for them to breathe. The underground water tank, bought used, was of sufficient capacity that with careful rationing and the addition of water from the pool the six of them could survive for over a year. The remaining credit on the new account was spent on a large propane tank which would supply fuel for both the cooking stove and the generator. The generator in turn powered the ventilation fans, the television and DVD player, the modem, the computer and a single light bulb in each of the rooms. The shelter's hatchway, with its extra-thick, double-insulated steel blast cover, was hidden beneath the hinged steps to the swimming pool.

He devised a homemade periscope from PVC pipe and mirrors, disguising its top within a corner of the doghouse at the back of the yard. Antenna wires for the AM/FM and shortwave radios and the satellite cable for the television and internet were run up through the same opening, through the doghouse and into the branches of the old sycamore tree above. It had been Mark's idea to route the periscope and the wires through the doghouse and to camouflage the antennae and the satellite dish in the tree, painting the wires and the dish to match the tree's bark.

Reginald thought back on the boy's ingenuity, smiling with pride. Unfortunately, there wasn't a single photo of any of the family in the shelter. Who would have thought that any photos would be needed?

He had been working on the project for close to two years when he was laid off from his job. Often fatigued and distracted from being up late at night on the computer, he had made several costly mistakes on large press runs, and when the company needed to tighten its belt, the less dependable became the more expendable. Being fired was enormously unfortunate—at least Reginald felt so at first, particularly given his concern over how Margaret was going to react—but after driving around town awhile, wondering what he would do next, he realized that he was relieved: he could now devote his full attention and time to the preparations.

Margaret, unsurprisingly, was exceedingly upset over the turn of events, and her frustration only escalated as her husband pursued new employment only halfheartedly and intermittently. But he had given up trying to convert her to his perspective on what the family's priorities should be, and she was barely talking to him any longer anyway.

At Ron's barbeques next door, Reginald could hardly help but steer any and every conversation to politics, world events and the economy. In any circle he joined, his dark and dire predictions would thoroughly dampen any of the festiveness, though certainly not the drinking. Even Ron, who was never at loss for words and seldom shied from an argument, would find himself laboring to change the subject to lighter fare whenever subjected to Reginald's dour expositions on what the future would bring. And so it was that, in the company of dozens of his neighbors, Reginald would often find himself standing or sitting quite alone—and he would slip quietly away to return to his shelter.

On the children's birthdays, he would make an appearance for just long enough to see the candles blown out on the cake before excusing himself to continue experimenting with the shortwave radio or studying his preparedness books. He thrived on reading about how to farm, how to skin and tan animal hides, how to conduct an emergency appendectomy, how to trap fish and how to distill water in the desert using only a square of plastic sheeting and some chopped-up cactus. He and Margaret were no longer sleeping together, which was just as well because he found that he slept more comfortably and securely in the shelter anyway.

Mark had become quieter around his father, and the longer his father went without employment, the quieter Mark became. Of his own initiative, he found a job bagging groceries at the supermarket, and despite his mother's protests he turned over the entirety of his meager paychecks to her to put towards the household bills. The store manager allowed him to bring home bags of dented canned goods, imperfect fruit and day-old bread.

After returning home from the store one evening, Mark came down the shelter ladder. Upon his father's asking, he claimed to have nothing particular on his mind. Reginald returned to working on his wish list for additional emergency supplies while Mark sat on a bunk and thumbed distractedly through one of the illustrated medical books, paying little attention to its contents.

What Reginald hadn't known was that when he had first told his son of his intention to build the shelter, Mark had envisioned a high-tech cave, a secret hideaway, an underground lair, and with such an asset at his disposal—a powerful counter to the money, athleticism and good looks of the other boys at school—he might have a chance of earning the notice of one of the prettier girls, maybe even Lisa Ashburn. In the two classes he shared with Lisa, who was not only pretty but smart, he could think of little else. While hefting the endless shovelfuls of dirt in the backyard, he fantasized of the possibilities constantly, wanting the hole to be as deep as he could dig it, imagining Lisa's eyes growing wider with each descending step and her reaching out for his reassuring hand. She would be so impressed with the facility that, there in the dark, wearing one of her soft, mounded sweaters, she would let him kiss her—and maybe even do other things.

Of course he had revealed none of this to his father, but now that the shelter was more or less finished, he finally worked up the nerve to ask—as his eyes continued scanning casually over the medical illustrations—if it might be okay if he showed the shelter to just one other person, as long as that person swore never to tell anyone, not even her own parents.

Reginald's explosive rebuke put his son immediately on the defensive, but when Mark tried to leave, Reginald physically blocked his path, stating that there was more to be said and more that would be heard. When Mark attempted to detour around him, Reginald grabbed him by the front of his shirt and pushed him all the way back into the sleeping quarters, shoving him towards the bunk on which he had been sitting. Mark stumbled. His head hit the concrete wall. He sat there on the bunk, drawing his knees up to his chin and clutching the back of his head as he stared at his father in pained disbelief.

The force of Reginald's verbal assault was commensurate with how deeply he felt betrayed. He expressed his profound disappointment that his own son could dare to even think of jeopardizing all they had worked so hard to build together by wanting to show it off to some slut at school. That was the word he had used. He knew it was harsh, and truth be told, he had no idea who the girl might be, much less the quality of her character—but in the end, it didn't matter: he simply *had* to convey to his son, through the sheer force of his own anger if necessary, that revealing the shelter's existence to *anyone* could be a matter of life or death for any and every member of the family, right down to the baby, and that no inconsequential, primped-up object of a teenage boy's hormonal urgings could be allowed to put at risk the family's survival and salvation. No one else could possibly matter—no one. He had to impress upon his son, as firmly as was necessary, the proper value hierarchy. He might not have been able to accomplish it with the boy's mother, but with his own son, he would not fail.

As Mark sat in silence, eyes averted, his father went on to lecture for a full hour—revisiting and reviewing every imminent threat that they faced and every extended consequence of taking a wrong step between now and the day that their lives would depend on their preparations. When he had finally exhausted his anger and arguments, he asked if he had made himself clear. Mark mumbled in the affirmative and asked weakly if he could leave. Reginald acquiesced only after securing another oath from Mark that he would never reveal the shelter's existence to anyone.

As the boy walked unsteadily to the ladder, one of his hands still pressed to the back of his head, Reginald noticed the blood between Mark's fingers. Feeling a momentary flood of shame and regret, he wanted to apologize, but said nothing, reminding himself that it was a hard lesson but a lesson that had to be learned. What he had done may not have been ideal, but it had gotten the boy's attention, and the boy would thank him for it someday.

Later, as he wiped the blood off of the rungs of the ladder, he steeled himself for Margaret's reaction. But her reaction never came. Apparently, Mark never told her about the incident. The boy did, however, slip into an impenetrable melancholy during which he spoke as little as possible to anyone in the family and his grades plummeted further. Even going to the shooting range was no longer of interest to him, especially relative to his new obsession: the bloody obliteration of the parade of human and alien targets in his video games. His father's next visit to the shooting range was alone.

Reginald continued preparing, assembling a thick binder of emergency plans with a red cover and separate tabs of line-item instructions and lists for each conceivable disaster, including flow charts dictating the chain of actions to be taken by each family member in each scenario—tornado, nuclear explosion, power outage, chemical spill, rioting, etc. At the beginning of a long holiday weekend, he lured the entire family, including the dog, down into the shelter, and he sealed the hatch above them in order to conduct a four-day test under emergency conditions.

This didn't go over well with Margaret. She not only had just discovered one of the bills for Reginald's credit card, but was scheduled to attend a friend's wedding shower that Sunday. Mark, smoldering, locked himself in the toilet closet and refused to come out until he was allowed to go back up to retrieve his game console. Reginald himself had to break his own rules the very first night, returning to the house to retrieve Martha's pumpkin pillow, without which she refused to sleep, and for formula and diapers for the baby. The cases of formula in the storage room were discovered to be past their expiration date, and the boxes of diapers he had purchased only six months prior were already a size too small.

The dog, Beezer, refused to do his business on the square of fake grass that Reginald had provided for the purpose, and it became unavoidably evident that the ventilation in the toilet closet would need to be improved. With six living and breathing mammals in such close quarters—seven, including the dog—it became clear that a dehumidifier would be necessary. Margaret insisted, in one of the few moments in which she was speaking to him, that at the very least a supply of spices and flavorings would be necessary for cooking and that his inventory of foodstuffs was entirely too carbohydrate-heavy for as little exercise as any of them could expect to get in a confined space over an extended period. After bathing and drying the children, dealing with their dirty clothes and wet towels turned out to be an unanticipated challenge.

In the morning, Margaret declared that the shelter was simply too cold and damp for the baby, with whom she returned to the surface. Mark pleaded to be allowed to go up with her, and when his request was refused, he retreated again into his games and comic books until Martha began pestering him incessantly to play cards or dolls with her. After he shut himself in the toilet closet again, Martha and little Peter began fighting over which videos they would watch and who had pulled whose hair first. The children barely touched the rehydrated stroganoff Reginald prepared for lunch, with Martha declaring dramatically that it made her want to throw up. After another nine hours underground, a propane leak in the stove's connection provided Reginald with sufficient cause to call an end to the first trial only thirty hours into what was supposed to have been a ninety-six hour stay.

Yet he emerged undaunted. He bought new board games that the family could play together and a preparedness-education kit complete with curricula, flash cards, projects and worksheets that would make more valuable use of the children's time. He purchased a second small heater, a dehumidifier and exercise videos which the family could all follow together to help the children burn off excess energy. In the toilet closet he installed a stronger motor for the ventilation fan. The gas leak on the line to the stove was soon patched, and to manage wet clothes and linens, he built a drying rack with a fan in the storage room. Once he had supplemented the pantry shelves with more canned vegetables, fruits and a spice rack, he was confident that Margaret should have no further complaints. Privately, he decided that in an emergency of any duration Beezer would have to fend for himself above: over the long term, the extra space for dog food and the additional water requirements simply couldn't be justified, and besides, carrying the squirming dog up and down the ladder was always a struggle.

A year and six days later, he cleared the fog from the lenses of his gasmask and looked back into the rooms behind him. The light from his headlamp swept through the sleeping room and over the empty bunks, all but one of which were still perfectly made, the pillows fluffed as if Margaret had arranged them only yesterday. He hadn't been able to bring himself to strip the sheets and the neatly turned-down blankets, having never given up hope that, somehow, someway, at least one if not all of his family would eventually make their way back to the shelter. But none of them had. It was small comfort to him that, in all likelihood, they had died almost instantly. Or at least so he hoped.

It was Margaret's fault, he thought again, and bitterly, for the thousandth time.

On that fateful Sunday morning three weeks after the first test, they had gotten into a fight again over priorities. The children's summer break was almost over, and he had announced at breakfast that, with only twenty minutes notice, the family was to retreat again into the shelter and spend a full week there.

At their silent, blank stares in reply, he enthusiastically shared news of the games he had purchased, the learning programs he had found, and the improvements he had made so that they would all be more comfortable, and how much fun it would be spending the week together learning how to weave rope out of dead plant fiber, make soap from ashes and leftover cooking fats, and fashion shoes out of a deer hide he had found at a yard sale.

Mark muttered something under his breath which to Reginald sounded like an expletive followed by the word "loser." He demanded that Mark repeat it and more loudly, which Mark did not. He demanded that Mark not leave the table, which Mark had already done. When he started angrily after the boy, Margaret pushed her chair back and stood, positioned conveniently in her husband's path. Something in her eyes gave him pause. She was studying him as if she had never seen him before.

She excused the other children from the table, and when all but the baby were out of earshot, she suggested to her husband that if he knew what was good for him and for the family then he would be spending the next week searching full-time for a full-time job, and not just searching but finding. Furthermore, when he wasn't job hunting, she needed his help cleaning the house and the garage, and then she wanted him to start converting the half of the garage where the supplies had been into a playroom, and then perhaps to lay out the raised vegetable garden that he had been promising her since before Peter was born. And furthermore, she wasn't going to spend another single day in "that wretched hole" until and unless he could produce nothing less than a category-F2 tornado on the near horizon or he installed a skylight and a soaking tub in it for her.

He stormed out of the front door. Mark was already disappearing around the far street corner on his bicycle. Finding a morning paper on Ron's sidewalk, Reginald brought it in, slammed it down on the table in front of Margaret and jabbed his finger at the headlines about the drug wars spilling over the southern border, the riots in Detroit over benefit cuts to public workers, the earthquake in Missouri and the corn and wheat shortages predicted by the end of the summer. What should worry her most—he was shouting now—was the report about the three Arab men seen photographing the nuclear plant in California. If she cared about her family, she would care enough to be prepared—or maybe she didn't really love the children as much as she claimed to. . . .

He had made a mistake with that last—he knew it before the words were out of his mouth—but there was no taking it back once said, and besides, maybe that was exactly what Margaret needed: to be shocked a little into being sufficiently worried about the seriousness of things.

After a long, chilled silence, she stated calmly that she was taking the children to the park, and that they would talk again that evening.

Reginald finished the remainder of his breakfast at the table alone, reading the paper, whistling to himself as he rinsed his plate. He took the truck to the discount store where he bought a half-dozen bags of bulk rice and took advantage of sale prices on batteries and sterile gauze. When he returned home, Margaret was still gone. He switched off the outside power to the shelter, clipped Beezer to the chain on the doghouse and went below, turning on his headlamp as he descended, to tinker with the wiring to the radio, which had been shorting out of late.

When he surfaced for lunch, Margaret's car was in the drive, but neither she nor the children were in the house. He guessed that they were likely over at Ron's. The music, lighthearted chatter and laughter wafting over the fence annoyed him. Beezer's whining and straining at the doghouse chain annoyed him. With a sandwich and soda in hand, he climbed back into the hatch and lowered the cover to block out the noise.

While attempting to create some slack in the radio's antennae wire, he fouled the satellite cable in the swivel of the periscope mount. After untangling the mess, he was glancing through the scope's eyepiece to ensure that it was turning freely again when a mushrooming ball of smoke and fire filled the horizon in the viewfinder.

The mirror in the periscope above shattered as a booming vibration shuddered through the shelter's walls and hot air rushed in through the pipe. A splinter of glass punctured his cheek—he had turned his eye away just in time. He stumbled back, tripping over the chair, and his soda can crashed to the floor as the antenna wires and cable ripped out of their connections and whipped violently up into the pipe, disappearing into the hole.

Regaining his footing, he tore off his shirt, broke out what was left of the eyepiece with a screwdriver and stuffed the shirt into the opening before racing up the rungs of the hatchway. At the top, he hesitated, suffering a moment of indecision before wrenching the handle tightly to seal the cover. He waited there, listening, hoping to hear something, anything, but no sound penetrated the thick layers of steel. There was only the silence of the shelter and the pounding of his heart.

His hands were shaking as he descended. As he started up the generator, he cursed himself for not thinking to locate the breaker from the outside power within the shelter itself—though it was probable that there was no longer any outside power available anyway. Switching on the ventilation system, he was thankful for having invested in the protective filters. To thoroughly seal the periscope opening, he stuffed a can of tomato paste into the pipe behind the shirt and fixed the plug into place with a layer of adhesive, capping it with a solid layer of duct tape.

His emotions careened from elation to agony, from fear to absolution. All of the risks he had taken, all of the calculations and the thousands of hours of planning and toil had paid off. Adrenaline surged through him as though he had just struck a mother lode of gold after mining in solitude for years—yet he was in a mortified panic for Margaret and the children. A terrible sense of helplessness and guilt enveloped him as he tore at himself over what to do.

He turned on the television, but there was no signal. Scanning the radio frequencies yielded nothing but faint, distant whispers and unintelligible garbles. Beneath the six feet of earth, cement and steel, the equipment was worthless without the antennae and the satellite. He checked his cell phone, though the signal had never penetrated the shelter when the hatch cover was closed, and it was unthinkable to risk opening the cover now: the toxic smoke and radioactive fallout might already have reached lethal levels. He had prepared for the cell-phone system being knocked out, insisting that each family member carry a two-way radio when traveling more than a hundred feet from the house, but it was unlikely that Margaret had hers with her in her purse—more than once he had discovered it in her nightstand. She complained that it was too heavy and took up too much room. There was a chance that Mark may have been carrying his radio in his ever-present backpack, but with the hatch cover closed there was no signal on Reginald's. After attempting to call several times on the pre-arranged channel, with no success, he left the radio on, propping it on the table, calling out on the other channels intermittently, waiting and hoping to hear any news at all, from anyone—but there was only flat static.

Yet he had prepared even for this contingency, given that an electromagnetic-pulse attack or a disruption in the atmosphere from a massive solar flare might knock out all radio circuitry and transmissions. As a final option, if anyone could make it back to the shelter, he had attached a small metal rod by a chain to the outside of the hatch cover. The family, even little Peter, all knew and had practiced the special signal: three quick taps, followed by three slow, then three more quick—Morse code for "S-O-S." A family member needed only to tap the code to be distinguished from an unwelcome intruder.

By the third day that no one had come knocking on the hatch, he was able to begin ruling out the less catastrophic scenarios. While it was possible that Margaret and the younger children could have been killed or injured in a more localized explosion, the friend with whom Mark had been spending time lived all the way across town, and if Mark couldn't come or send authorities to help by now, then it could only be concluded that the entire town had likely been destroyed or contaminated. Anyone daring to venture out into the open under such conditions could receive a lethal dosage of radiation within minutes, maybe even seconds. He owned a handheld radiation detector, but it was worthless for testing the levels outside the shelter unless he dared to open the hatch cover, which only a fool would do.

A week went by, and then a second week, with no sound from above. With each day that passed, Reginald's confidence grew that the worst scenario had indeed occurred. If the blast had been due to terrorists or an enemy nation attacking not only the local plant but the hundred-plus others across the country, along with perpetrating god-only-knew what other forms of attack—then chaos, horror and despair would reign above. It would be anarchy or martial law, and it was hard to say which would be worse.

If only Margaret had taken him seriously. If only she had listened.

He still missed his wife and the children, but there was only so much worrying that a man could do. He found himself humming and whistling as he went about his days.

He had been right.

During the third week, someone or something knocked firmly on the hatch cover with something larger than the little metal bar. It sounded more like a hammer. After a silence, the knocking came again and louder—but certainly not using the special code. By the time the third set of knocks came, slower, louder yet and more insistent, Reginald was pointing his loaded rifle up at the hatch, with the safety off, wondering how long it might take for someone to break in. But the knocking ended, followed only by silence. It could have been anyone—a representative of the new police state, a Chinese soldier, an armed thug. He tossed in his sleep that night, dreaming that a starving, subhuman scavenger, its face and body half melted away by radiation, had pried through the cover and was clawing at his face. Pieces of its rotting body fell off as he tried to swat it away.

Over the following months, the occasional odd sound could be heard through the plumbing and ventilation pipes. He imagined several times that he heard a male voice and children laughing, but he knew from the books that such hallucinations were not unusual when one is sensorially and socially deprived. There were a few pictures and videos of his family on the computer, but he had no way to print them out, and after the computer terminally crashed during the second month underground, he was left with only his memories. There were several dozen movies in the shelter, and though most were the children's animated films and cartoons, he watched them all, many times over, until the DVD player started skipping, and then froze, and then died. There was no manual in the shelter for repairing a DVD player. He took it apart and put it back together, to no avail.

He stripped the wire from the player's electrical cord and attempted to snake a makeshift antenna up through the ventilation pipes, but he couldn't get anything through or around the blast valves. The short-wave would occasionally whisper or crackle with what might have been voices, but it would pick up only a few faint signals now and again. One night, he strung the wire as far up into the hatchway as it would reach and managed to find a station on which he could barely distinguish what sounded like someone making an angry speech, in Portuguese perhaps. A somber voice on another station slowly intoned a long list of numbers in French. He listened to it for hours. The only other station that came through was broadcasting what sounded, weakly, like Arabic music. While evidently there was still life somewhere on the planet, the indications didn't bode well for conditions above.

By the end of the fifth month, he detested every type of freeze-dried and powdered food in the pantry. He had never been much of an epicure, but now he craved fresh meat, fruit and vegetables, real bread—and Margaret's cooking. He suffered insatiable cravings for hamburger and steak. But the key to survival was patience and determination.

After re-reading all of his preparedness books, he calculated, as well as he could manage, how long it might take for the radiation to settle out given the prevailing winds on the day of the blast and the distance from the plant. It was possible, maybe even probable, that the radiation may have returned to survivable levels within a few weeks or months, but the threat from desperate survivors in the ensuing societal collapse could prove every bit as dangerous or more so. After filling half a notebook with contingencies and flow charts, he concluded that he should remain underground for one full year before he could feel safe exposing himself on the surface. To the target date he added six days: civilian predators or enemy soldiers might anticipate that survivors would emerge on the exact anniversary date. It would be better to wait until they were less alert. Further, he planned to surface at two in the morning, when those who might be monitoring the area would be least likely to notice him. He marked the days off on the wall calendar, and after his phone battery gave out, he measured the time by a wind-up alarm clock.

After six months underground it became necessary to begin rationing the propane. Despite the ground's insulation, he had felt interminably cold through the winter months, and by early spring he had burned through more than three-quarters of his fuel supply trying to stave off the chill. To compensate, he began limiting hot meals to one every other day and warming only enough water for bathing once every two weeks.

During what was likely the first snow melt above, he started noticing the water seepage. At first there were only a few damp patches along the hairline fractures which had developed in the concrete floor and walls, but it wasn't long before there was standing water in the storage room. It was possible that he had miscalculated the water table or the necessary drainage around the shelter, but he had guessed at it as best he could, unable to risk bringing a professional onto the property for consultation. He was able to keep up with the leaks for a while, mopping up the water with rags and pumping it out through the plumbing—until the plumbing backed up and he couldn't unclog it, which with the rising water resulted in sanitary challenges and a pervasive noxious odor that made mealtimes even more unpalatable.

The water from the storage tank had begun to take on a strong, metallic taste, so he switched to the pool access, but the water from the pool was green and brown with algae and had small brown worm-like creatures floating in it. The standing water in the shelter seemed the least unpalatable option of the three. When he ran out of chlorine for water purification, he resigned to boiling, which only increased the humidity in the space and depleted the propane supply more quickly. Soon, there was six inches of standing water, then ten.

The fuel in the propane tank was depleted in the ninth month, leaving only a twenty-pound emergency tank and the remaining supply of batteries for power. He saved the emergency tank and rationed the batteries, using them only in a single flashlight and for only two hours a day, which provided just enough light by which to read and to eat his cold meals. For the remaining twenty-two hours, he lived in complete darkness, with no heat and no flame for cooking. He tried once to start a small fire with scraps of cardboard and a wooden crate, and nearly died from smoke inhalation before being able to assemble and don a gasmask.

Even without smoke and carbon monoxide from a fire, the air in the shelter had become woefully stale. Without power, the filtration and ventilation fans were inoperable, and he could only hope that any remaining radioactive material above had settled enough that he would survive whatever might carry down through the pipes. So far, his detector registered little radiation within the shelter itself.

In the tenth month, he stopped washing his clothes and gave up bathing altogether. From moving about in the cold water, his feet had become red, numb and blotchy, and were giving off an odor of decay. The medical books indicated that he had probably developed trench foot with significant potential for the onset of gangrene, for which there would be only one option if he wished to continue living. He read several sources on amputation, but had doubts as to whether he would be capable of amputating one or both of his own feet. Thenceforth, he did his best to keep them dry, swabbing them with alcohol. For navigating through the shelter above the water level, he distributed crates, food tins, inverted buckets and the bushel bags of seeds, which were already rotted and worthless.

By the eleventh month, he was coughing often and painfully, having developed what he suspected was a bronchial infection, and an abscess in one of his molars was swelling his jaw, making it nearly impossible to chew on the right side of his mouth. There was no means of obtaining the herbal palliatives touted in his home-remedy books. He might have put whisky on the tooth to ease the pain, but his one bottle of spirits had been consumed within the first two weeks underground and the bottle of rubbing alcohol had been depleted cleaning his feet. He was losing weight, no matter how much he tried to eat.

Through it all, he remained committed to the goal. He had come this far—he would stay below for the full year and six days. Better sick than dead, he repeated to himself in the darkness, over and over again. But the last months in the shelter were a psychological and emotional hell, with only the two hours of light a day and his mind playing tricks on him. He was sure he heard sirens wailing one night; then he wasn't sure of it at all. Half of the time, he couldn't tell if he was awake or dreaming and he would lose all sense of time and place. Sometimes he was certain that his family was there underground with him, and he would go to their bunks and talk to them and try to wake them. Sometimes they would be alive and would talk back to him. Other times he would find them dead and he would cry for hours. More than once, in the pitch dark, he was certain that he could see the baby, floating facedown in the water. There were hours on end when he was sure that the water was filled with writhing snakes. He would have long arguments with Margaret over what color they would paint the house when they surfaced again, and Ron would be in the kitchen barbequing hamburgers and hotdogs in the dark and insisting that Reginald couldn't have any until he went to the store for mustard, relish and beer. The smell of the sizzling meat tortured him. He once came to his senses realizing that he had just spent what could have been an hour or a full day combing the shelter for his truck keys.

He vacillated between feeling dejectedly suicidal and euphorically messianic. At one moment he would have the loaded handgun at his temple with a trembling finger on the trigger, and at the next he would be relishing the prospect of having a community of doting followers at his beck and call when, like Jesus, he would emerge from his tomb, alive, purified and sanctified from his ordeal. He was finally able to pry out the abscessed tooth, but the open socket remained infected— the source, he believed, of his fevers. His feet and lower legs itched horribly and unrelievedly, and his cough only worsened, leaving his throat painfully raw as he spat up droplets of blood into his hand.

But finally, the appointed day came.

He used the emergency tank of propane to start the generator one last time for light, hot water and a hot meal. He shaved so that there would be no leaks around the gasmask from his beard, and he bathed from head to foot before putting on his last pair of clean clothes, which had been saved so as to present a trustworthy appearance to other survivors. A good first impression could mean the difference between being embraced or being shunned or worse, depending on the new standards and conditions above.

As he had never bothered putting a crate or upturned bucket in the bottom of the shaft itself, being that he never spent anytime there, getting to the ladder meant sloshing through the water, which filled his boots—but on this day, it couldn't have mattered less to him.

As he stood at the base of the shaft, he turned and took one last look at the squalid, flooded rooms behind him. Then looking up, he readjusted the gasmask, zipped up the hazmat suit and checked to make sure that his pistol was secure in its holster on his waist. After taking a deep breath—which brought on another fit of coughing, fogging the lenses again—he began to climb.

He was in such poor physical condition that the climb of merely fourteen feet exhausted him, particularly with the water-filled boots. At the top, the hatch cover was stuck so thoroughly that he feared he wouldn't be able to open it at all. Panicking, he envisioned his slow death alone in the shelter, but with repeated, urgent pounding with his shoulders and back, he finally broke open the seal.

Quivering with the anticipation of seeing the moon and stars again, hoping that the night sky wouldn't be overcast, he raised the cover a mere slit—and was blinded by the daylight streaming in. He had miscalculated the time of day. Either his clock was inaccurate or he had failed to wind it during one of his deliriums—but now that the hatch was open, he no longer cared. Exposing himself as little as possible, he pushed the radiation detector through the slit and squinted through the gasmask's fogged lenses to read the meter. The reading was normal, possibly even lower than the level in the shelter below. He tapped at the detector's case, wondering if the batteries were still good, contemplating for a moment going below to search for any fresh batteries he may have overlooked—but his curiosity and desperate longing for the surface drove him recklessly upwards and out.

The hinges of the hatch cover screamed loudly as he struggled to raise it. Once vertical, it was too heavy and he was too weak to keep it from falling open and clanging loudly against the pool decking. Drawing his pistol, he crawled out and onto the ground, the water spilling from his boots. He crouched, waiting and ready.

Clumps of waist-high grass and patches of brown weeds had grown tall in the yard. The house and the pool still stood, though both were in deplorable condition. The pool's cover was torn, faded and lying half on the ground, and the back screen door of the house hung only by its lower hinges. There were boards over the windows. The sycamore tree behind the pool appeared to be undamaged, along with the satellite dish still camouflaged in its branches, but the doghouse was lying on its side against the back of the house, trailing a tail of antenna wire and broken PVC pipe. Pieces of his periscope jutted from the ragged hole where the doghouse had once stood.

Half of the wooden fence closest to Ron's house lay on the ground, snapped off near the bottom, revealing Ron's hedge. The hedge, in contrast to the vegetation in Reginald's own yard, was fully green and neatly trimmed. As he was contemplating how oddly out of place it appeared, a spray of water from over the top of it hit his gasmask squarely, flooding the filters. He fumbled the pistol and it fell, clanging, down the shaft. Coughing and sputtering, he ripped off the mask and sucked in the fresh air.

"Hey, sorry about that! Didn't realize anyone was over there. Who . . . Oh my god—Reginald? Is that you? You look like hell, man! Where have you—? Oh. My. God. . . . Hey, Wendy—come over here! It's Reggie!"

Ron's wife appeared at his side and stared at her neighbor, dumbstruck.

"Reggie," Ron continued, "tell me you haven't been down in that shelter for this past whole year."

Reginald stammered, "But you didn't know . . . Nobody knows . . ."

"Jesus, Reggie—the whole neighborhood knew. Kids talk, you know, and Margaret *had* to talk to somebody, and besides, what the hell else would you have dug that big hole for, with all your doom and disaster talk—a wine cellar?"

"Margaret? She's alive? The kids . . . ? But why didn't anyone . . . ? Where are . . . ?"

"Montana. They moved to Montana. The longer you stayed down there, the madder she got, and I figure it was September or so when she started seeing Steve. You know, Steve—from across the street, the engineer who worked at the nuke plant. The company is building another plant up north, and she and the kids moved up there with him just after Christmas. Don't worry—the kids love him. He's a great guy. Gotta say, Margaret seems pretty happy too. Oh, and hey, sorry about the house."

"The house? What about the house?"

"Right—you wouldn't know. The bank finally foreclosed on it last week. Which is just as well—it's become a real eyesore. Bringing the neighborhood property values down, you know. They'll have it cleaned up in a jiffy though."

"But, the explosion . . . the plant . . ."

"Explosion? What explosion? The only explosion there's been around here was last summer when I blew up the barbeque. Both tanks, sky high. What an idiot I am, huh? Always a good idea to check the connections before playing with the igniter, right? You should have seen the fireball, Reggie. Damned lucky no one was hurt. Hey, sorry about your fence—I offered to rebuild it, but Margaret said to let it lie, said she enjoyed getting a little extra light and fresh breeze through the back yard. Man, you should have seen your dog though! The bang scared Beezer so bad that he dragged the dog house all the way across the yard. We laughed about that for months, didn't we, hon?"

Wendy finally found her voice. "You look famished, Reginald. We just grilled some steaks. I'll bring you over a plate." She disappeared in the direction of her kitchen.

"Must be a pretty sweet setup you got down there, Reggie, to be staying down there for a whole year. . . . But you're white as a ghost, man."

Reginald didn't respond. He was staring at the back door of what used to be his home.

"Well," Ron continued, scratching his head and squinting at the hazmat suit, "I'll be getting back to my watering then. Wendy will be right over. Let us know if you need anything."

When Ron had gone, Reginald sank to his knees. Then he fell back onto the earth, his arms falling open and wide. His eyes closed as the sun began burning his face.

*   *   *
*

If you enjoyed these stories and poems, please consider supporting the author's work by telling your friends and by submitting a review on Amazon. Thank you!

For the latest Cordair fiction,
please visit the author's website at

www.quentcordair.com

To alert us to any errors or typos in the text, or to submit any comments, compliments or suggestions, please send an email to **dobby@cordair.com**. Thank you for your assistance!

About the Author

Q UENT CORDAIR was born in 1964 in southern Illinois. He
was raised "under a church pew," as the saying went, in a
fundamentalist Christian sect, and though his family moved regularly—the grass always being greener—it would nearly always be to a
town with a church of their denomination close by. It was an insular
community in which the devout were forbidden the enjoyment of
movies, pop music, television, school sports, alcohol, jewelry, makeup,
skirts shorter than knee length and most other temporal pleasures
worth mentioning. It may not be a coincidence that the writer and
artist now resides and works in Napa, California—the heart of the
wine country—where with his wife, Linda, he enjoys some of the
world's best wine and food, and owns an art gallery brimming with
lovely nudes and other sensuous delights. When not painting for the
gallery, he writes romantic, adventurous fiction that celebrates a

markedly different perspective of life on earth than the one under which he was raised.

While many things in his youth were proscribed, the reading of fiction was not—an oversight, no doubt, by church authorities—for it was amidst the library shelves that the eyes of a young man were opened to a marvelous and exciting world beyond the church's walls. He immersed himself in boys' mystery books and was captivated by the stories of Stevenson, Defoe, Wyss, and Doyle. In his mid-teens, he was discovering the dramatic tales of Fleming, Follet, Sienkiewicz and Hugo, and would soon bask in the ingenuity of O. Henry and the genius of Ayn Rand.

At seventeen, he enlisted in the United States Marine Corps with the goal of becoming a career fighter pilot, but by the time he was accepted to attend the U.S. Naval Academy, he recognized that the only work that could ever truly satisfy him was the creation of the kind of visions that had inspired him through his youth. After completing his four-year enlistment, he launched his writing career.

His first short story was published in 1991 by the Atlantean Press Review. To support himself while writing, he waited tables, took employment as a security guard, stocked groceries and worked the graveyard shift at a mail-processing center. While working a desk job at an auction firm, he began seeking paying work more in line with his artistic proclivities. After teaching himself how to paint, he began taking portrait commissions while working at his easel in a local park and would soon be exhibiting at art fairs.

The Quent Cordair Fine Art gallery was opened in 1996 in Burlingame, California, where the work of other painters and sculptors of like vision were offered in addition to Quent's own portraiture, figuratives, landscapes and still lifes, which are now collected by an international clientele. Linda assumed management of the business as it continued to grow, with the square footage doubling in 2006. Yet even this space proved to be too small, and in 2008, the Cordairs moved the gallery to a 3600 square-foot location in downtown Napa, where today they offer the finest selection of Romantic Realism in the world. Quent's present efforts are devoted to his writing: in addition to publishing his short stories, he is completing a novel of grand scope inspired by his life's journey and passions. The author can be found on Facebook and at his fiction blog, "As It Should Be," at www.quentcordair.com.

The Cordairs live in Napa with their cats, Lexie and Sadie, and their border collie, Mollie.

$*$ $*$ $*$
$*$

Author's Website

"As It Should Be"
www.quentcordair.com

On the cover...

Lunch Break

An original oil painting by Quent Cordair.
60" x 84" oil on canvas.
© 1996, Quent Cordair. All rights reserved.

"Her body pressed against the rise of stone beneath her, a young woman enjoys a moment's respite on a high ledge above the city, at one with this place carved from the earth, a place made for her, by her—her home."

Limited-edition giclée prints on canvas
Signed and Numbered by artist & author Quent Cordair

30" x 42" Signed & Numbered, Limited Edition of 95
20" x 28" Signed & Numbered, Limited Edition of 95

Available at ~

Quent Cordair Fine Art

The Finest Romantic Realism
*In Painting & Sculpture * Est. 1996*

1301 First Street, Napa, California 94559
(707) 255-2242 * **art@cordair.com**

www.cordair.com

97163624R00090

Made in the USA
Columbia, SC
15 June 2018